Harmony & Choas 3
A Jersey Love Affair

Harmony & Chaos 3
Copyright © 2017 by Reds Johnson
Interior Design Formatting | Strawberry Publications, LLC

ISBN-13: 978-1722720063
ISBN-10: 1722720069

READER DISCLAIMER!!!

This book contains flashbacks from book one and two of Harmony and Chaos.

Acknowledgments

Let me first say thank you God for helping me push through and finishing this final book. Also, a BIG thank you to my mother Maria Ward for encouraging me, and motivating me along the way. It took a lot out of me to complete this finale. To all the readers that supported this series, THANK YOU! Thank you goes a long way, and I will forever be grateful for the support that I get. Peace & Blessings to all, and stay tuned for more from me, only this time I'm bringing **Reds Johnson** back!

-IAmRedsJohnson

#ISlayBooks

Order Of Books To Read In This Series:

Harmony and Chaos

Harmony and Chaos 2

Sincerely, Harmony

Harmony and Chaos 3

Sincerely, A Real One: Chaos Response

Sincerely, Harmony 2

Recap: Harmony & Chaos 2

Chaos Miller & Harmony Winfield-Miller

It was going on 4 p.m., and Chaos was sitting on the couch, waiting for Harmony to get in. He saw her leave out that morning but hadn't heard from her since, and he grew to be concerned when Brave called him and let him know that something had went down between Jasmin and Harmony at the boutique.

He wasn't upset at her for not telling him because Brave also told him that she didn't want to worry him because he was still in the process of recovering. Chaos was looking through his phone when he heard the knob being messed with. He knew it was Harmony and, when she walked in, she was stunned to see him waiting for her.

"H—hey babe. I didn't expect to see you sitting there," she stuttered.

"Yea. I decided to stretch a little. I spent too much time in bed. But, enough of that. What happened between you and Jasmin at the boutique?" he asked, getting straight to the point.

Harmony dropped her purse by the door and walked over to the couch to sit down. She was so overwhelmed that, when she sat down, she placed her face in the palms of her hands and broke down crying.

"Baby, what's wrong?" Chaos was concerned. He pulled her close to him and hugged her tight. Despite the mishap they went through with Chaos confronting her about possibly cheating, it didn't stop the fact that she was his wife and she needed him right then and there.

"I can't do this anymore. I just can't," she cried.

"Do what? Ma, tell me what's going on. Whatever it is, you know I'll handle it," he told her.

Harmony buried her face in his neck. "Somebody tore the boutique up. I mean, they trashed it. I'm so tired of fighting Chaos."

By now, Chaos was heated. He didn't like to see Harmony cry and he didn't like to see her hurting. He gave her the money to open her store, but her blood, sweat, and tears were put into it, so the fact that somebody took it upon themselves to fuck up something they didn't own or put money into had him livid.

"Dammit, Harmony, why the fuck didn't you call me?" he asked.

"I called the police and made a report, but I didn't want to worry you Chaos. You've been through enough."

"I don't give a fuck what I've been through. You're my wife, and I'ma protect you and make sure you good at all cost. Regardless of what I'm going through, you come first," he told her.

Harmony cried more as Chaos talked to her. She had betrayed him so much and, here, he was unaware of it all and still being a good husband.

"Stop crying baby. I'ma handle all this shit, believe that," he said as he gently removed himself from her embrace.

Chaos headed upstairs and quickly put some clothes on, along with his crème Timberland boots, just in case he had to stomp somebody to the ground. He rushed back down stairs and grabbed his keys off the table.

"Chaos, where are you going?" Harmony asked.

"I'm going to ya store to see what's going on and what I can find out," he explained.

Harmony got up and rushed over to the door where she dropped her purse when she first came in. She opened it and pulled out the letter she wrote to Chaos.

"I need you to read this," she said, as she walked over and handed it to him.

Chaos grabbed it and looked at it strangely. "What is it babe? Is it important because I need to go like now?"

"Yes, please read it," she begged.

"I got you, ma. Just let me get shit squared away at ya store and I'ma read it as soon as I can. I promise," he said and kissed her all while putting the letter in his pocket.

Harmony kissed him back but it felt so different, considering she had been giving herself to another man for over a month.

"I love you," she said.

"Love you more ma," Chaos responded before making his way out of the house.

She closed the door behind him and made sure he got in his car safe. Once she saw him pull out of the driveway and pull off down the street, she went to sit back down on the couch. Harmony grabbed her cellphone from beside her and went to her text messages. She clicked on Kaotic's name and scrolled through their old and recent conversations. She cried and shook her head at the same time.

"This shit was never worth it!" she screamed.

It was time that she ended the affair she was having. She had told Chaos the truth and, once he finally read the letter, she knew that she would be in for a rude awakening. She wanted no parts at all with Kaotic, and what they had going on was now the past.

Harmony: *Look, we can't do this shit anymore. I'm done with you and I'm done with this. I can't believe I stooped so low and allowed myself to step outside of my marriage and do the things I did with you. I don't care what kind of control you think you have over me, but this shit stops today. I even ran into your little girlfriend today. You could've told me that you and Jasmin were together. My reputation is skating on*

thin ice because of your no-good ass! I told Chaos everything, you son of a bitch. Lose my number!

Harmony felt relieved after she sent Kaotic that text. She felt like one of the weights had been lifted off her shoulders. Now, all she had to do was wait until Chaos read the letter, so they could be on the journey to fixing their marriage, that was if he decided to stay with her.

***

Chaos Miller

Chaos was pissed at the sight of Harmony's boutique. There was *do not cross* tape everywhere. He ripped it down and went inside. He couldn't believe the events that had taken place in such a short time. First, he got shot and then Harmony's store got trashed. He wondered if there was any connection between the two.

He looked around at everything that was damaged before heading to the back. He walked into Harmony's office, which was trashed as well. Not as much as the outside, but her desk was kicked over and there were papers thrown everywhere.

As Chaos continued to look around, he noticed the security cameras were still intact and indeed still on, and he got excited.

"Dumb ass muthafuckas," he smirked.

He reached up and began to go through the videos. The more he watched, the more he realized he was getting more than he bargained for.

Chaos put his hand over his mouth, in shock at what he was seeing. He couldn't believe that he had just witnessed Harmony letting another man fuck her. He watched, as the man picked Harmony up and fucked her as if she was his woman. Harmony had ample chances to stop the situation but, from the looks of it, she was enjoying the dick down that Kaotic was giving her.

Hurt wasn't the word that could explain how Chaos was feeling. Chaos couldn't remember a time he ever cried, but he couldn't help the tears that had formed in his eyes. His stomach was in knots, and his mouth watered as if he needed to throw up. He was broken at that point because besides his mother, Harmony was the only other woman he trusted.

He trusted her and loved her enough to make her his wife, and this was what she did in return. He left the streets alone, not only to better his life, but because he wanted to make sure Harmony lived the life she always has.

Chaos was well aware of the image Harmony's mother painted him out to be, and he wanted to prove to her that he was the right man for Harmony. He would have never thought that his assumptions would come true. He loved Harmony to death and he would have put his life on the line for her at any given moment. The only thing he could think of was the conversation he had with Harmony about what he would do if he found out that she was cheating on him.

I'ma kill you repeated over and over in his head, as he removed his hand from his mouth and balled up his fist.

June 5th, 2010

Harmony and Chaos

The Beginning

Twenty-one-year-old Harmony Chardonnay Winfield had just gotten off the NJ Transit bus in front of the hood's famous mini-mart Coastals. It was just hitting 3:00 p.m., and she was more than tired. She had just gotten off work, which was at Rue 21, a fashion store for women that was located inside of the Cumberland Mall in Millville, New Jersey. It was hot, she was bothered, and all she wanted to do was grab a bite to eat and head straight home.

She slung the backpack that she carried around with her over her shoulder and sighed loudly, as she walked across the small parking lot and headed for the store door. Harmony was in mid-step when she stopped and moved to the side because someone from the car beside her had thrown something out of the window. She looked to her right and saw a fine specimen of a man licking a cigar.

"Excuse you, sir," she said to him as she cocked her head to the side as if she was checking in, but she was really checking him out the entire time.

Chaos looked to his left to see where the melody of a voice was coming from. "Yea? You need somethin' ma?" he asked.

"I need you to stop littering. You threw that wrapper out the window and it hit my foot," Harmony rolled her neck and folded her arms across her chest as she spoke.

Chaos cocked his head to the side and chuckled as he licked his lips. He continuously licked the cigar as he eyed her. Chaos couldn't front; he most definitely enjoyed the view of her slim but curvy frame. Harmony was looking damn edible to Chaos, just by the way her smooth Melanin skin was glistening in the sun.

"I don't think I said anything funny," she challenged.

"Never said you did," he chuckled once more before putting the blunt between his lips, picking up his lighter, and putting fire to the end of the weed-filled cigar. He took a few pulls, inhaled, exhaled, and then coughed.

"What's ya name beautiful?" he asked.

She gave him a once over, as if she wasn't interested knowing she damn sure was. "Harmony, and yours?" She still gave off attitude, but Chaos thought it was cute.

"The one and only Chaos, baby."

Although his response came off cocky, Harmony could tell that he was by no means like that in any way. Chaos' entire demeanor came off as boss like, and she didn't gather that by what kind of car he was driving. He just seemed like the type of man that knew where he came from and understood where he was going. He was a hood nigga at its finest, but Harmony could see the potential in him, and that was all it took. From that day forward, she had fell in love with a thug, and at a young age at that. Although some didn't agree with it, that was just one thing out of many that made her love him harder.

Chapter One

Chaos Miller

Chaos was in awe; his mouth was covered with one hand, and he stuck his other hand in his pocket as he tried to gather his thoughts. When he stuck his hand in his pocket, he hit something. While the surveillance videos were still playing, he pulled the paper out of his pocket and realized it was the letter Harmony told him to read. He began to read what Harmony wrote him, and the tears that had formed in his eyes fell freely.

I'ma kill you repeated over and over in his head, as he removed his hand from his mouth and balled up his fist.

Chaos was fuming as he finished watching the surveillance videos. He crumbled up the letter and shoved it back in his pocket. He couldn't believe that Harmony would betray him the way that she did.

Although he assumed that she was cheating, he never would have thought his assumptions were true. Never in his life would he have thought that he would witness the love of his life fucking with another man, and a guy he had seen around a time or two before.

"I'ma fuckin' kill her!" Chaos growled, while storming out of the office.

Chaos wanted to do more damage to the store. He wanted to burn the motherfucker down to the ground but, after seeing the words *whore, slut,* and *homewrecker* written on the walls, he knew he didn't need to do much more of anything because Harmony's karma was coming around tenfold.

He left out of the store, and all he could see was red as he got in the car. Barely closing the door good before starting the car, Chaos peeled off down the street. What was usually a fifteen to twenty-minute ride became a ten minute one. Chaos burned rubber as he peeled into the driveway of his and Harmony's home. He turned the car off but left his keys in the ignition, as he got out of the car.

Harmony was still sitting on the couch sobbing when Chaos stormed into the house. She didn't even have to ask what was wrong because the rage in his eyes let her know that he'd read the letter.

"Cha—"

That was the only words Harmony got out before Chaos took off towards her. Harmony got up in the nick of time and hopped over the arm of the couch and put her hands up in defense. Chaos leaped over the couch, grabbed Harmony by her throat, and slammed her up against the back wall.

Harmony clawed at Chaos' hand as she gasped for air. She couldn't get a word out because the grip he had on her neck was so tight.

"Bitch, I should fuckin' kill you in here! You gon' cheat on me wit' another nigga in the muthafuckin' shop I bought you!"

Slam!

Chaos slammed Harmony up against the wall, causing picture frames to hit the floor and shatter.

"C..."

Harmony tried to speak as tears ran down her face. She was beginning to get lightheaded and, for a second, she actually thought this was the end. She was so sure that Chaos was going to kill her right there in their living room but, unexpectedly, he let her go.

She slid down the floor, holding her neck and gasping for air. "I-I'm s-orry," she whimpered.

"Fuck you! Fuck that! You ain't sorry!"

Thump!

Chaos punched a hole in the wall as he stood over her. Harmony ducked for cover, as if he was hitting her; her hands were over top of her head, protecting herself from whatever was to come.

"I'm so sorry baby," she cried as she looked up at him.

His eyes were closed but, when she said she was sorry, his eyes popped open, and Harmony was looking death straight in the eyes. The look in Chaos' eyes was cold and deadly. His eyes were stone-cold black and the sclera was completely covered by the darkness of his iris; his pupils had decreased and Chaos looked possessed. In the blink of an eye, Chaos maneuvered so swiftly, as he grabbed a fistful of Harmony's hair and his Beretta off his waist simultaneously while pointing it to her head.

"Baby, please!" Harmony screamed. "I'm sorry!"

Tears were running down her eyes, and beads of sweat had formed across her forehead. Chaos had never been so angry at her before in the entire time they had been together, and she had never been so scared for her life. The man she had fell in love with since day one was now pointing a gun at her head, as if he didn't know her at all.

Her heart felt like it was about to explode through her chest because of how fast it was racing. She could feel her bladder finally give out and she was now sitting in a puddle of urine, but that was the least of her worries.

"Please," she cried once more.

A part of her felt like Chaos was just trying to prove a point and let her know not to ever pull a stunt like that again, but then another part of her knew that the love he had for her was sparing her life because if she was anyone else, her brains would have been splattered on the wall behind her.

"Shut the fuck up, bitch! Please what? Huh? Please what?" Chaos pressed the barrel of the gun to her head. "You didn't give a fuck about me when you was fucking that nigga! You ain't give a fuck about me when you was fucking that nigga in the shop I

16

bought you. You ain't give a fuck about me when you continuously fucked that nigga and, now, you pregnant! Bitch, I should kill you right now!"

Chaos had never called Harmony out of her name before but, right now, she wasn't the woman he met six years ago, nor was she the woman he married. Right now, she was just like the rest of the women he had run across back in the day, and the street code was no women, no kids, but being a grimy ass male or female crossing him could only leave you one way, and that was six feet under.

***

Kaotic Miller

Harmony: *Look, we can't do this shit anymore. I'm done with you and I'm done with this. I can't believe I stooped so low and allowed myself to step outside of my marriage and do the things I did with you. I don't care what kind of control you think you have over me, but this shit stops today. I even ran into your little girlfriend today. You could've told me that you and Jasmin* *were together. My reputation is skating on thin ice because of your no-good ass! I told Chaos everything, you son of a bitch. Lose my number!*

Kaotic reread Harmony's text message repeatedly. He was angry and satisfied all in one inside because he knew that Chaos was now mentally broken. Without even responding to Harmony's text, Kaotic scrolled through his contacts until he came across Chaos' number. He smirked as he sent the pictures he had taken of Harmony's face, nude body, and swollen pussy.

Kaotic: *I'm sure you gon' enjoy these pictures bro, and I'm not using that term loosely. You have a beautiful wife, and I'm glad we both got the chance to experience what a lovely fuck she is.*

Once Kaotic finished texting what he needed to say, he hit the send button and placed his phone back down on the table, as he reclined his chair and put his hands behind his head in a relaxed manner.

***

Chaos Miller & Harmony Winfield-Miller:

Ding! Ding!

Ding! Ding!

Ding!

With the gun still pointed at Harmony's head, Chaos' phone had gone off several times. His phone ringing was the least of his worries, but his mind instantly thought of his mother and something being wrong.

He eventually let go of Harmony's hair, but he kept the gun pointed at her head while he reached in his pocket and grabbed his cellphone. He had several text messages from an unknown number. Chaos touched his screen to unlock his phone and he clicked on the notifications.

Once again, Chaos was taken aback, and he wasn't prepared for what he witnessed. His chest burned and it tightened up from anger and hurt. He tried his hardest to keep the tears that had formed in the corners of his eyes in. Not once had he ever been so tempted and afraid to shoot someone all in one but, after seeing the inappropriate pictures of his wife, the woman he made vows with until death did them part, he had no other choice but to let one off.

Pow!

Chapter Two

Renee:

It was 5 p.m. on the dot, and Renee hadn't heard from Harmony since she'd left her place. She wondered was she okay, and if she had told Chaos about what happened at the boutique. She shook her head as she replayed the events that had happened earlier that day. Renee was happy that she finally got a chance to whoop Crystal's ass but, more so, she couldn't believe that Harmony had stepped out on Chaos.

Although Harmony had made such a terrible mistake, Renee still looked up to her. She knew that Harmony loved Chaos with everything inside her and she was praying that, when Chaos did find out about what Harmony had done in the past, he could forgive her and work on rebuilding their marriage.

Since Renee had met Brave and spent more than enough time with him, she could imagine the four of them going out and painting the town with fun. Two boss ass Queens and two boss ass Kings was how she saw it. All Renee could do was hope for the best.

***

Harmony Winfield-Miller:

What was once a puddle of urine was now mixed with watery shit. The smell had damn near fumigated the entire living room. Harmony's face was covered in tears, and snot dripped from her nose. Her hair was a complete mess, and her heart fluttered rapidly. She looked at Chaos' smoking gun from the corner of her eye.

"Please," she cried.

Her face was ugly with fear, and all Chaos could do was lower the gun. He wanted to kill her so bad, but the love he had for her wouldn't allow him to take her life.

"I hate you with everything in me, bitch. I swear, from this point, on we're done. Don't say shit to me, don't ask me for shit, and don't call me for shit. You better be glad you ain't got no family because ya ass would be the fuck up outta here!"

Chaos' words cut Harmony deep, as she watched him put his gun back in the waist of his jeans. He stormed out of the house, slamming the door and making the house shake violently, causing Harmony to jump out of fear.

"I'm sorry," she whimpered once more.

Chapter Three

Crystal & Jasmin:

"I can't believe that trick ass hoe hit me. Like she really tried to embarrass me out there." Crystal shook her head as she looked in the mirror of her huge marbled-styled bathroom.

After the fight with Harmony and Renee, Crystal decided to stop by her house to get herself together and have a drink or two. Jasmin was too busy still sobbing over the fact that Kaotic cheated on her with Harmony, a woman she'd envied since she met her.

"Bitch, what the fuck are you crying over? We just got our asses whooped, and you over there boo whoo'n," Crystal snapped.

Jasmin got up from the couch and went into the kitchen. She grabbed a few paper towels to dry her eyes, and then she walked back into the living room.

"I just can't believe he would betray me like this. After all we've been through, he decides to go and sleep with my boss? Like really? Did I really deserve such treatment? I can't stomach what happened, and the nerve of this bitch to put her hands on me. Like, I had every right to confront her the way that I did. She was sleeping with my man, and I wasn't having that whatsoever," Jasmin explained.

Crystal rolled her eyes as she continued to look in the mirror. She had just about had it with Jasmin's old grandmom acting ass. She looked in the mirror once more, before peeking her head out in the hallway.

"Oh, bitch, cry me a fucking river, why don't you? Have you seen your damn face? It looks like Kaotic betrayed you a long time ago. I don't care how much you may have annoyed him. No woman deserves to get beat on, and he whooped your ass because he cheated on you." Crystal shook her head in disgust. "I swear, a nigga will stop trusting you because he cheated."

"Kaotic had his reasons for hitting me, I don't mind that. What bothers me is he cheated on me with Harmony. I can't forgive him for that, and then that bitch had the nerve to put her hands on me as if I did something wrong?"

Crystal motioned her arm upwards and shut the bathroom light off and walked out into the hallway. She reached the living room and folded her arm across her chest as she leaned over, putting the majority of her weight on her left leg.

"So, you can forgive him for hitting you, but not for cheating? Girl, you can't be that stupid?"

Jasmin gave her a shocked look. She didn't like the way Crystal had been coming at her since she'd heard about the situation.

"I may be emotional right now, but I think you need to watch how you're coming at me. I am no child of yours," Jasmin's tone was firm.

"Well, that's exactly how you're acting, like a child. You are a grown ass woman; hell, you're older than all of us and you're letting this dude beat on you and treat you like shit! That's unacceptable and I honestly don't wanna hear you crying over him all day, especially since we just got our asses beat in public!" Crystal's voice got louder with each word she spoke.

She didn't give Jasmin a chance to respond. It was going on 7:15 p.m. and she needed a drink bad.

"I'm about to shower and, when I get out, I'll fix us some drinks. While I'm in the shower, you need to get your shit together because I refuse to allow you to sit in my house crying over a no-good ass nigga." She waved her off as she walked down the hall and into her bedroom.

Jasmin shook her head while taking out her cellphone. She scrolled through her contacts until she came across the cab's number.

Ring.

Ring.

"Hello, Jaylene's taxi."

"Yes, can I get a cab to..."

***

Brave & Chaos Miller:

Brave was relaxing in bed while watching the club on the cameras at home and waiting for Renee to respond to his text. It was a Friday, but it was the first night that he decided to see how Coroner, also known as Big C, could handle the club while he nor

Chaos was there. So far, things were going well, and Brave was definitely impressed with the way he went from security guard to CEO in a matter of hours.

He made a mental note to speak to Chaos about it and maybe even move him to a higher position. He knew that would be a major power move because the three of them were one lethal combination.

Knock.

Knock.

Knock. Knock.

Knock. Knock.

Bang! Bang!

Bang!

Brave heard loud knocking that turned into banging, which caused him to quickly sit up and grab his gun that sat on the nightstand. He wasted no time sliding over to the other side of the bed and leaving out of the bedroom. He walked down the hall with quick steps, but eased up once he got to the door. Brave peeped through the side window and was surprised to see who was standing on the other side.

"Damn, bruh, you had me ready to-"

Brave stopped in mid-sentence when he saw Chaos' face. He could tell that he had been crying, and he knew something was wrong. But, before he could ask, Chaos had already revealed the problem.

"She cheated on me. Harmony cheated on me."

Brave's mouth fell wide open. The only thing he could do was tuck his gun in his waist and embrace the man he knew as his brother in a heartfelt brotherly hug.

Chapter Four

Crystal:

What was supposed to be a shower turned into a hot bath with Epsom salt and aroma therapy. Crystal had a long day, and her body was sore from the beat down she got from Renee earlier. By the time she got out of the bath, got dressed, and wrapped her hair, Jasmin was gone. She briefly searched the house, but she was nowhere to be found.

"I know that bitch ain't get in her fucking feelings and leave," she spoke out loud.

Crystal went to the bedroom and took out her cellphone. She called Jasmin's cellphone, but she was sent to voicemail on the second ring. By now, she was furious because in her eyes, Jasmin had no right to leave unannounced. Crystal felt disrespected because she didn't feel as though she did anything wrong. The only thing she was trying to do was put

Jasmin up on some game, but it was clear that she was set in her own ways.

Crystal: *Bitch, I like how you waited until I got in the shower to leave. You really on some pussy ass shit, and I don't got time for it. If you wanna be a dumb ass bitch and continue to deal with a man that don't want shit to do with you, then be my fucking guess. But, from this point on, I'm done with ya old has-been ass!*

***

Harmony Winfield-Miller:

Harmony had finally found the strength to get up from the shitty and pissy spot she was sitting in. She slowly walked into the kitchen and went into the cleaner cabinet. She bent down and grabbed the bleach and twisted the cap off, while she walked back into the living room at a slow pace.

Splash!

Harmony poured the bleach on the mess she had made and twisted the cap back on. She walked away and put the bleach on the glass coffee table and headed upstairs. Although she was the only one in the house, she was still embarrassed because of the condition she was in at that moment.

Once she made it to the bedroom, she quickly went into the bathroom and turned on the shower. She got nauseous by the foul smell coming from her body and clothes when she took them off. Before getting into the shower, she leaned down and reached for the bag that was in the small trashcan. After taking the bag out, she put her entire outfit inside and tied it up, throwed it on the floor, and climbed into the shower.

She allowed the hot water to hit her body as a fresh batch of tears ran down her face. She couldn't believe the events that had taken place within the last few hours. Her world and marriage came crashing down on her all at once. She couldn't deny that it was indeed her fault, but she also felt as though Chaos should take some responsibility in what went on.

All she ever wanted was more of his time and attention, but it seemed like he was married to the club instead of her. Harmony knew that she was wrong for stepping out on Chaos, but it was as if she had an outer body experience. Everything that she was doing that was wrong felt so right and, every time she was around Kaotic, it felt like she was the only girl in the world, at first.

After several minutes, Harmony got her wash cloth and lathered it up good with some Dove body wash. She scrubbed every part of her body with force. Harmony felt so dirty, and the bathroom had a weird smell to it due to the scent of her body wash and the awful smell of her shit and pissy-stained clothing that she had taken off.

Harmony washed up three times before allowing the water to hit her body for several minutes, before turning the shower off and getting out. She grabbed her robe off the back of the bathroom door and put it on. Afterwards, she looked into the mirror and wiped the steam off and she immediately broke down crying, as she looked at her swollen, puffy, red eyes.

"I'm so sorry, Chaos," she spoke, as if he was in the room with her.

Harmony wiped her face and left out of the bathroom, but not before grabbing the bag full of dirty clothes. She went downstairs and headed directly in the kitchen to throw the bag in the trash and, once she was done, she grabbed the mop bucket and filled it up with hot water. When the bucket was filled halfway, she turned the water off and grabbed the bucket out of the sink. Harmony took the mop off the wall that sat on one of the hooks that Chaos had put up for her convenience and headed back into the living room.

She dipped the mop in the hot water, rung it out, and began to clean up the mess she made a little while ago. Harmony dipped the mop back in the bucket and repeated her steps all over again, until the floor was clean to her perfection.

Once she was finished, she put everything away and plopped down on the couch. She saw her phone lighting up, so she grabbed it and looked at the notifications. Harmony scrolled through her missed calls and text messages, and they all were from Renee. As bad as she wanted to lay on the couch and sulk in her own misery, she knew that the best thing to do was to call Renee back and invite her over. At that moment, she needed a friend's shoulder to cry on.

Ring. Ring.
Ring.

"Hello? Harmony, are you okay?" Renee asked as soon as she answered the phone.

Her concern caused Harmony to break down again. She couldn't control the tears that began to fall from her eyes and wet her face.

"Harmony, please tell me what's wrong? What happened?" she asked.

"He, he got so mad. He just snapped on me. Our marriage is over. It's officially over," she cried.

Renee sighed deeply. She hurt for her friend, but she knew Chaos was going to find out sooner or later and, when he did, it wasn't going to be pretty.

"Did he hit you?" she wanted to know.

Regardless of what Harmony did, if Chaos hit her, Renee was going to come shut shit down. It wasn't her place but, considering she had a past of abuse of her own, she refused to see someone she adored as a friend go through it as well.

"No, he didn't hit me," she snorkeled. "But, if he did, I couldn't blame him. He was just so upset, and I... I...."

Harmony couldn't continue; the tears and emotional distress had her breaking down repeatedly.

"Just calm down Harm," Renee said.

Harmony shook her head no. "I can't calm down!" she screamed.

"Then, what do you want to do?" Renee asked.

"I want my husband back! This shit got out of hand, and I can't just let us end like this. Chaos is my husband, and I refuse for him to just leave me as if he never loved me in the first place. I just feel so, so..."

Harmony burst into tears once again, and all Renee could do was listen to her. She could imagine how both Harmony and Chaos felt because she had been on both sides of the fence before. She was once the one getting cheated on and once the cheater.

Chapter Five

Brave & Chaos Miller:

Brave sat down and looked at the man he saw as a brother for many years, break down over the woman he loved unconditionally. He didn't know where to start or what to say. All he knew was that Chaos was hurting, and he was hurting bad. He knew something fishy was going on with Harmony, but he didn't want to assume the worse. Now that Chaos had revealed that Harmony cheated on him, he didn't feel bad for thinking the worse because his assumptions were accurate, but he never brought that to Chaos' attention.

"Look bruh, I know you don't wanna talk about it right now, but just know I'm here," Brave assured.

Chaos sat on the couch with his legs apart, and his elbows planted on his thigh as he held his head down and rubbed his head back and forth in a stressed manner. He was beginning to get a migraine and, the more he tried to come up with an explanation as to why Harmony betrayed him, he was only making himself more upset.

"I can't believe she did this shit," Chaos managed to speak.

It all seemed so unreal to him. The woman he took vows with until death did them part had betrayed him to the upmost.

"How did you find out?" Brave was curious to know.

Chaos removed his hands from his head and sat back on the couch and slouched down.

"The fuckin' security cameras in her shop and, on top of that, the nigga text my phone and sent me pictures of her, bruh."

Brave was confused. He couldn't understand what dude in his right mind would be bold enough to reach out to Chaos and do something of that nature. Furthermore, he couldn't understand why Harmony would be so selfish and disrespectful to put her and someone else's life in danger. He knew that Chaos might've been uncomfortable talking about the situation, but he had to get to the bottom of it, so he could help him figure out a solution. It wasn't going to be easy, but he was going to do all that he could to be there for Chaos during this rough time.

"What exactly happened? I mean, when the fuck did she get the time to pull some fucked up shit like this? And pictures? Pictures of them together?" Brave was confused. He was asking all sorts of questions.

Chaos shook his head as he glanced up at the ceiling. He fought back the tears as they tried to force their way out. He couldn't remember the last time he cried about something, but Harmony had snatched his soul out of his chest, and the emotions that were running through his body was uncontrollable.

"Somebody fucked her shop up. From the looks of things, it was the bitch who nigga she fucked. She came home crying and shit, and Harmony is my heart, so you know I panicked a little." Chaos shook his head again before he continued telling Brave how shit went down.

As bad as he didn't even want to touch basis on the situation, considering it just happened, he couldn't see himself not letting the man he looked at as his brother know what was going on. Brave had been there through many tough times, and he had witnessed many things that may come off as embarrassing to some, but he stuck it out with Chaos.

"I told her I was gonna go to the shop and see what shit was lookin' like. So, I get there and the shit got *do not cross* tape around it. I go inside and the walls got writing on them, you know, typical female shit."

Brave nodded, and Chaos continued.

"I go to the office and shit knocked over, but no major damage. You know me; I went straight to the security cameras like I been tellin' her ass to check from jump, but she never listens. Anyway, man, I check them and she was fuckin' the nigga right in her shop."

Brave's mouth fell open. Harmony was bold as hell to pull something like that in the store Chaos paid for. What she did was beyond disrespectful, and Brave was surprised that Chaos didn't put hands on her or, better yet, kill her.

"Damn, that's some fucked up shit. Sis buggin'. Like she dead ass on some fuck shit for that shit. Man, that's some crazy ass shit," Brave said.

He was more than disappointed in Harmony. She was supposed to be Chaos' rider but, instead, she was out fucking another nigga while Chaos was constantly working, trying to make sure they were straight for life.

"The nigga sent me naked pictures of my wife, bruh. My wife. She ain't even use a condom wit' him," Chaos began to choke up.

Brave was at a loss for words. There was nothing he could say to what Chaos had just revealed to him. Harmony had reached an all-time low, and he was going to have a word with her very soon.

"I know you hurtin' right now bruh and, to be honest, I don't even know what to say to console you at this moment. One thing I do know is that I'ma help you get through this. Believe me, you know what I've been through, so I can relate to ya situation a little," Brave said.

He watched the silent tears roll down Chaos' face and all he could do was sit there in pure silence, as Chaos attempted to release some of the hurt he had just experienced. As he sat there, Renee crossed his mind, and he wondered how much did she know about the whole Harmony stepping out situation.

Brave wasn't stupid by far, and he knew that the mysterious little call Renee had with Harmony earlier had something to do with what was going on. He respected her loyalty, but he wondered how much Renee was capable of when it came to hiding things and keep secrets.

Chapter Six

Harmony Winfield-Miller & Brave & Renee:

Knock. Knock.

Knock.

Ding. Dong.

Ding. Dong.

Knock. Knock.

Knock.

It was Saturday morning, the first of April, when Harmony heard banging on the door. She never made it to the bedroom due to her emotional state, so she passed out on the living room couch the night before. The banging was so loud, it scared her, so she jumped up in a frantic stated. She quickly rubbed her eyes and got up off the couch.

Harmony walked at a fast pace to the door; she looked through the peep hole and saw Brave standing on the other side. She inhaled and exhaled deeply.

"This is not going to be good," she said to herself as she slowly unlocked the door. She had only cracked the door open a little when Brave Bo guarded his way in.

"That shit you did was fucked up!" he snapped as soon as he pushed past her. He glanced around the house as if he was looking for something or someone.

"What are you doing, Brave?" she asked.

"Ooh nah, don't worry about what I'm doin'. The question is what the fuck you been doin'? You really fucked another nigga, sis? Shit, should I even call you sis? Because right now, I don't know who the fuck you are!"

Harmony covered her face with her left hand. She expected Brave to confront her, but she just didn't feel like dealing with him at that moment.

"Brave, now is not the time for this. I'm really not in the mood for any of this to be honest."

Brave raised his eye brows and leaned back in a shocked manner.

"You ain't got time for what? You had a lot of time to start dealin' wit' another nigga, and you damn sure had a lot of time to fuck the nigga. So, now you tellin' me you ain't got time? Fuck outta here Harmony! You know that shit was foul as fuck. My bro wouldn't have ever did you like that. Not only did you cheat, but you betrayed him, his loyalty, his trust. In the shop he bought you! That's some fucked up shit, and you know it!"

Brave gave zero fucks about how Harmony felt. He loved her as his little sister, but he be damned if he stood by and allowed her to get away with the way she did Chaos, the man he looked at and known as a brother for many years. They struggled together, hustled together, and came up together so, in his eyes, it was only right that he had his back, no matter the situation.

"You don't think I know that!" Harmony broke down in tears. "I fucked up Brave! I can't take that back, but I don't need you coming over here riding down on me. I got enough shit on my plate."

Brave waved her off. He didn't give a fuck about her tears because she clearly didn't give a fuck about Chaos. He couldn't understand her actions, and why she would do such thing.

"Fuck outta here wit' that bullshit Harmony. Six years, bruh? Six fuckin' years down the drain, for what? For a piece of dick? You know how much pussy Chaos is around daily? Bitches come at his neck daily at the club, and he shut them straight the fuck down because he know what he got at home. None of them bitches compared to you, Harmony. You're his everything, and you do this to him? That's fucked up, and I know my brother hurtin' because this the second time I ever seen him cry."

Tears rushed down Harmony's face. Hearing Brave tell her that Chaos was crying crushed her soul. She never meant to hurt him. She was already upset with herself for allowing her and Kaotic's situationship to go that far. Harmony knew she allowed her selfish ways to get the best of her, but she didn't need for everyone to get involved and place the blame on her, although it was very much her own fault.

"It wasn't supposed to happen like this. I fucked up, I know I did, but I don't need you coming here telling me that," she sniffled.

"I don't give a fuck what you don't want me doin'. I'ma do the shit regardless because what you did was fucked up. Ain't no comin' back from this Harmony; like, you fucked up big time, and you need to be thankful that he didn't kill ya ass, especially after that nigga sent pictures of you to Chaos. And you ain't use a condom? The fuck wrong wit' chu?" Brave was highly disappointed in Harmony. All he could do was shake his head as he read her from head to toe.

Tears poured from Harmony's eyes as she listened to the words that came out of Brave's mouth. She knew that she had fucked up, but Brave confirming that she was lucky to be alive scared her something serious.

"I fucked up, I know I did, but..."

Knock. Knock.

Knock.

Harmony was interrupted by the knocking at the door. She wasn't expecting anyone, so she thought. Brave immediately grabbed his burner off his waist and looked at Harmony, as he waited for her to answer the door. In his mind, the nigga that she was cheating with was stopping by, so he was going to shoot his ass first and finish asking questions later.

Harmony had never given Kaotic her address, so she wasn't worried about him popping up, but her stomach became nervous when she had an instant flashback of the bitch Brittany coming to her home. She quickly wiped the tears and put on her boss face because she was ready for anything the bitch brought her way.

She slung the door open and, to both her and Brave's surprise, it was Renee.

"Damn, what the hell did I walk into?" she asked.

Brave had his gun out and Harmony had a nasty scowl on, as if she was ready to rip something apart. They both seemed to sigh a sigh of relief when they saw it was her.

"My bad, I forgot that I told you to come over," Harmony apologized.

"It's cool. You know I had to come by and check up on you. How you holdin' up?" she asked.

Brave unintentionally waved his gun back and forth. It was in his hand, and he was confused at how they were standing in front of him trying to hold a normal conversation.

"Nah, nah, fuck all that girly shit. What the fuck are you doin' here?"

Renee really didn't pay attention to Brave being there; her main concern was seeing if Harmony was okay but, now that her focus was straight, she didn't want to run into him.

"I just came to see Harmony because she wasn't feeling well, that's all." Renee didn't necessarily lie; she just didn't tell the full truth.

"Fuck outta here wit' all that. You ain't just pop up to check on her. What the fuck you know about what's goin' on?" Brave asked, while still waving the gun back and forth.

"First of all, you need to chill and stop waving that fucking gun at me. Secondly, I just came to check on my friend, that's all. I don't know what the fuck you talking about." Renee rolled her eyes and spoke with much attitude.

Renee didn't know she had Brave fucked all the way up, but she was about to find out. One thing about Renee was that she didn't give a fuck how hood you were; her mouth was reckless and she had the hands to back it up.

"Who the fuck is you talkin' to? Renee, don't fuckin' play wit' me because the way I'm feelin', bitches don't mean shit to me. It ain't nothin' for me to let one off up in this bitch, so I suggest you tone that shit the fuck down before it be more problems than a muthafucka!"

Renee rolled her eyes once more, but she didn't say another word because both her and Harmony knew that Brave wasn't playing around. She kept her mouth shut and turned her attention to her homegirl.

"Harmony, are you okay?"

"I don't know Renee. I really don't know," she responded.

"Brave, can you put that damn gun away?" Renee asked.

"Nah, I think I need to keep this shit out until I find out what the fuck is goin' on," he stated seriously.

"What are you talking about now?" Renee threw her hands up in the air as if to say 'really'.

"I asked you a muthafuckin' question. What the fuck do you know about what's goin' on between Harmony and Chaos?"

"I told you I don't know shit!"

Renee refused to tell Brave about her knowing that Harmony had cheated on Chaos, got pregnant, and didn't know who the father could be. She was loyal, and she couldn't find herself snitching and causing Harmony to be in more shit than she already was. She liked Brave, but they weren't together as of yet, so holding back this bit of information wouldn't hurt anything.

"So, you just decided to pop up out of nowhere, huh?" Brave wasn't convinced at all.

"Nigga, I don't gotta prove shit to you! I told you I came over here to check on my friend! I ain't heard from her, so I had every right to stop by and check on her! Stop coming at me sideways like that!"

"Yo, who the fuck-"

"Stop! Just stop!" Harmony screamed. "Brave, Renee didn't know anything about me cheating on Chaos, okay. It was all my doing and I didn't get anyone else involved for a reason. I fucked up, I fucked up my marriage, and, right now, all I want to do is get my mind right so I can fix things with my husband."

Harmony couldn't hold back the tears. She had been crying all day yesterday, and all that morning, but she was even more emotional to see Brave and Renee arguing over her fuck ups. Her intentions weren't to have things go as far as they did, but it was clear that what happened had spiraled out of her control. She couldn't believe that all this bickering was over who knew what about what she was doing.

"Fix what? You keep sayin' fix it, when the shit you did ain't forgivable Harmony! My nigga is hurtin', and I mean hurtin' bad. This shit ain't gon' be just a walk in the park," Brave said to her.

"Do you gotta talk to her like that? I mean, I don't know what's going on, but I know you ain't gotta come at her like that," Renee added.

"Renee, I ain't for none of ya shit today. You think a nigga stupid, when I know you know what the fuck is goin' on and, like I said before, the shit ain't gon' be no damn walk in the muthafuckin' park!" Brave put his gun back in the small of his waist and pushed past both ladies.

He slammed the door a bit when he left out of the house, but it wasn't enough to startle them or make the situation more than what it actually was.

"You okay girl?" Renee asked.

Harmony shook her head no. "My husband left me. I'll never be okay."

Chapter Seven

Harmony Winfield-Miller & Renee:

Sunday morning arrived and Harmony had spent most of it on her knees in front of the toilet throwing up. For the last week, she had been completely sick to her stomach, and now the drama between her and Chaos was causing her to have double the morning sickness.

"I can't do this, Renee. I just can't do this," she cried.

Renee was standing over Harmony, rubbing her back as she puked into the toilet. The smell was horrific and damn near burning her eyes, but she stuck it out and held her friend down.

"Harm, you gotta pull yaself together. I know this is a fucked-up situation, but look at you. You look like shit and been lookin' like shit for the past week."

"How can I get myself together? My life is fucked up. Everything is fucked up! Renee, I'ma fucked up person who did some fucked up shit." Harmony was crying so much that she puked again.

Renee shook her head at how bad Harmony fell off. She understood the situation, but sulking in her own misery wasn't going to solve anything, nor was it going to get her husband back.

"What the hell do you mean how can you get yaself together?" Renee was confused.

This wasn't like the Harmony she knew and grew to love as a sister and best friend. She put her hand under her chin and pulled her face towards her.

"Remember what you told me? That you go through shit too, but it's all about keeping it together. You gotta be a woman on her boss shit out here. If you're going to weep, then do that shit behind closed doors. Never let anyone see you sweat! Not these bitches or these niggas! Granted, you're doing this behind closed doors, but let's not forget that fight. You gotta keep ya shit together Harmony." Renee grabbed some tissue and wiped Harmony's mouth. "Like you told me that night, the shit stops and it stops now. Life is too short, and sulking in your

54

misery is not what we gon' do. If you plan on being friends with me, then I'ma need for you to step it up. Be a woman with confidence. Love yourself and, regardless of whatever it is that you go through, always make sure you pick yourself up and dust yourself off. Sis, now is the time to do just that. Pick yourself up and dust yaself off. Get ya business back up and runnin' and get your husband back by all means."

A fresh batch of tears rolled down Harmony's face. Those were some of the same words that she had spoken to Renee the first night the hung out at Centerfolds. It was like déjà vu because now, she was the one falling apart over a man whom was her husband.

"I hate to say it, but you're right. I can't believe you just used my own words against me, but I must admit, I needed to hear them," she sniffled.

"Well, sometimes a person can give advice but can't take their own until they're put in a situation to where they need to," Renee stated.

Harmony silently agreed. She pulled away from Renee and flushed the toilet. Once she was finished, she took some all-purpose bleach cleaner and cleaned up everything that didn't get inside the toilet when she was puking up everything she'd taken down. Harmony then brushed her teeth and washed her face. When she was done, she paused for a second as she looked in the mirror.

She had truly lost herself in the last month or so, and the disappointment and hurt was written all over her face. This wasn't the boss ass woman she was molded into. She didn't know the woman who was looking back at her.

"I'm too much of a boss to let this shit break me. I been through too much, and this is just another lesson learned. Yea, I fucked up, but it's time to get back on my shit, handle my business, and make shit right," Harmony coached herself.

A big smile spread across Renee's face. She was proud to see Harmony realize that she was in a fucked-up state of mind, and it was time to get out of it.

"That's right bitch! What's ya last name?"

"Miller, bitch! I'm the one and fuckin' only, and ain't no bitch gonna take my spot. Chaos will forever be mines and, after I get my shit together, we will be back together!" Harmony was back and in full effect, and Renee was loving every bit of it.

Clap! Clap!

Clap!

"Yesssssss bitch! Now, get yaself freshened up, so we can call a few people to get over to the shop to have that shit fixed up asap. We need to get some new arrivals for the week and plan a sale. It's time to get shit poppin'!" Renee was geeked and ready to make moves.

Harmony was feeding off Renee's energy, and it was much needed. While Renee left out of the bathroom, she took a quick shower and got dressed. For the remainder of their Sunday, they made phone calls to Armando to get his crew together to fix the shop by Monday, planned a sale for Wednesday through Friday, and even ordered some new arrivals for the following week. However, the entire time they were on their boss shit, Harmony's mind couldn't stay off Chaos. She knew they were over, but she couldn't wrap her mind around them being officially over. They had put in too much time with one another for that to happen and, one way or another, Harmony was going to get Chaos back.

***

Casey Miller & Chaos Miller:

Casey walked out of the laundry room and was heading down the hallway and into the dining room to fold up her clothes. She sat down at the table and placed the basket on the floor but, before she could begin to fold the shirt, she had picked up the movement from the doorknob caught her attention.

Her mood went from calm to nervous in a split second but, when she saw Chaos walk through the door, she sighed a sigh of relief.

"Oh, my gosh, honey, you scared me. It's not like you to use your key," she said.

"Sorry ma," Chaos said dryly.

Casey could tell that something was wrong with her son. His appearance seemed dull and unusual, and the vibe he was giving off wasn't the normal positive and productive Chaos Miller that she knew.

"What's wrong baby?" she asked as she put the shirt back in the basket and stood up, kicking the basket to the side.

When she got closer to Chaos, she could see that his eyes were puffy, as if he had been crying all night.

"Nothing, allergies ma," he lied.

A mother knows their child and, right then and there, Casey knew damn well that wasn't no damn allergies.

"What happened? Is Harmony okay? Chaos, talk to me," she said.

Chaos walked over to the counter top and leaned on it, rubbing his head in a stressed manner.

"She cheated on me, man," Chaos blurted out.

Casey grabbed her chest, as if she was short of breath. Her gut told her that Harmony and Chaos' marriage was in jeopardy, but she didn't feel like it was her place to say too much of anything.

"Don't jeopardize what you have, just because you have a messed-up past."

Casey remember the words she spoke to Harmony back when she was staying with them until Chaos was back one hundred percent healthy.

"I'm so sorry Chaos. How do you know?" she asked.

"Security cameras at her boutique, the letter she wrote me, and the nigga had the nerve to send me nude pictures of her. He had to get my number from out of her phone while she was sleepin',” he explained.

“Baby, I am so sorry. I tried to talk to her when I was staying with you all, but I guess it did nothing,” she said.

Chaos removed his hand from his head and looked at his mother strangely.

“What you mean you tried to talk to her? You knew she was cheatin’?” he asked with a disgusted look written all over his face.

Casey sighed as she thought back on the day Harmony flipped out when Brittany came by. It was just an innocent visit to most but, to Harmony, it was disrespect and, considering she was doing dirt, she assumed Chaos was too. Casey, on the other hand, knew Brittany was madly in love with her son and would stop at nothing to get him.

Knock. Knock.

Knock.

Chaos was interrupted by the knocking on the door. He got up from the table and headed into the living room to answer the door. Brave followed, but he took a seat on the couch while Chaos answered the door. Chaos wasn't expecting anyone that early in the a.m. When he opened the door, he was surprised to see Brittany standing on the other side. She was looking beautiful as ever with her all-black skinny jeans on, a tight white button-down shirt, and some all-white Steve Madden stilettos.

"What the hell you doin' here?" Chaos asked in disbelief.

Brittany took a step back. "Wow, thanks for the greeting," she said sarcastically.

"My bad but, foreal, what are you doin' here Brittany?" he asked again.

"I've been calling you and I haven't been getting a response. I got worried and I decided to stop by to see how you were doing," she explained.

"Aw shit," Chaos heard Brave say.

He looked back and saw Harmony standing on the staircase.

"What the fuck is she doing here?"

"Good morning would be nice," Brittany said with a pleasant smile.

"No, an ass whopping would do just fine," Harmony said as she came down the rest of the stairs. She walked over to the door and attempted to push past Chaos, but he held her back.

"Get the fuck off me, Chaos, because you dead ass wrong!" Harmony snapped.

Brittany was standing there in such an unbothered manner, and that pissed Harmony off even more. She didn't know what was going on between her husband and the woman that stood before her, and she became livid.

"You got this whore ass bitch coming to my home? Move the fuck out of the way, so I can split her shit!" Harmony screamed.

Casey came running down the stairs during all the commotion. Brave sat back on the couch watching Harmony flip out, and he shook his head because she had never acted that way before.

"Brittany, please leave," Chaos said.

Brittany nodded and turned to walk away. Harmony reached for a vase that sat on a wooden table next to the door and chucked it past Chaos' head, hitting Brittany in her back and shattering the vase.

"Harmony!" Chaos yelled.

Brave jumped up and moved Casey to the side, so she wouldn't get hurt in the process of Harmony's outburst. He grabbed Harmony by the waist and tried to help Chaos control her; meanwhile, Brittany had kicked off her heels and was charging back to the house.

"This bitch got me fucked up!" Brittany screamed as she started swinging wildly.

"Bitch, fuck you!" Harmony screamed as she tried to break out of Brave's grasp.

Both women were swinging but hitting everyone but each other. Harmony managed to get her hands on another vase, but Brave grabbed it before she could throw it.

"Harmony, calm down!" Brave said seriously.

"She better calm down before she get fucked up!" Brittany threatened.

Harmony heard that and tried her hardest to wiggle out of Brave's arms.

"Brittany, leave! Damn, just get the hell away from here!" Chaos said in frustration.

"Fuck you, Chaos! I don't need this shit!" Brittany spat as she turned away. She bent down

and picked up her heels before getting in her car and pulling off violently.

"Harmony, calm the fuck down! I'm not gon' tell you again!" Chaos warned.

"Fuck out of my face. You fuckin' that bitch, ain't you?" she questioned.

"No, I'm not! What the fuck is wrong wit' you!"

Harmony finally got out of Brave's hold, and she turned around and pushed him.

"Get the fuck off me!"

Brave held his hands up, as if to say he didn't want any problems.

"Harmony, what is goin' on?" Chaos asked again.

"I fuckin' hate you! That's what's going on!" Harmony said before pushing past him and running up the stairs.

Casey stood back in awe at the situation that had just taken place. She was an old woman, but she was also wise enough to know that Harmony was lashing out because of her own demons that she was facing.

Casey shook her head no and sighed again when she came to.

"I assumed something was going on, but I had no proof. Being an old woman, I can only go by what I see and the vibe I get. When a woman wants time, she will go over and beyond to get it, and I know this from personal experience."

"Why you ain't say somethin' ma?" he asked.

"I said all that I could to you that day because I wasn't sure of anything. I told you that you loved your wife and that was okay. What did you expect from me, Chaos? Did you want me to say I thought Harmony was cheating?"

"Hell yea! You could've warned me or somethin' ma, damn."

Chaos shook his head back and forth.

"Now, wait a goddamn minute. You watch your mouth when you're speaking to me. I wasn't sure of anything. I mean, yea, my gut told me that something was going on, but I wasn't sure what. I just knew that you and Harmony were distant from one another. I prayed and prayed for you both, but what was done in the dark surely came to the light. I'm sorry that you're hurting right now, Chaos, I truly am. But, you cannot and will not put the blame on me."

Casey was right, and Chaos felt like shit for accusing his mother of being the cause of him being unaware of what Harmony was doing. He was looking for a way out of the pain he was feeling, and his actions right now seemed justifiable in his eyes.

"My bad," he said.

"I know you're hurting right now. Believe me, I know the feeling. When your father cheated on me, it was like the whole world came crashing down on me at once. I didn't know what to do or how to handle the situation. I felt like I did something wrong at first. Like, maybe I wasn't pleasing him or maybe he wasn't happy with me. I was just a confused mess at the time, but then I realized that your father had his own life to live. Just because we made vows and said 'I do' meant nothing," Casey spoke as she went back to sit down at the dining room table. She picked up the shirt she was about to fold before Chaos walked in and proceeded in folded it. "You know, people need to realize that marriage is just a piece of paper. It doesn't hold much weight because a man or woman is going to do what they want to do regardless."

Chaos went from being slouched over on the counter top to standing up straight. He walked over to the dining room table, pulled out a chair, and sat down. He rubbed his head, which had begun to hurt due to the oncoming stress from discussing Harmony's infidelity.

"How can you say that ma?" he asked.

"I'm sorry to be so blunt baby, but this has been happening since the old days. Men would be married and have an entire family on the outside. Don't take that to the heart because I was just giving you an example. However, marriage is a precious thing, but it's not something that's permanent. Don't ever think that just because you're married that your heart is safe, and that's just the bottom line.

Chaos listened to his mother speak some real wise words to him. No matter how painful it was to hear them, he still listened.

"So, you sayin' she never loved me?" he asked.

"That never came out of my mouth, did it? I said don't ever think because you're married that your heart is safe. I believe that Harmony loves you with everything in her. I believe that she even loves you more than she loves herself."

Chaos looked at his mother like she was crazy because now, she was speaking in riddles and she wasn't making any sense to him. How can someone love you but still cheat?

"How is that possible when she cheated on me?" He wanted to know.

"Let me tell you something baby. Your father loved me with everything in him. That man would tear this city up if something were to happen to me. Hell, he ever tried to fight my doctor one time because I caught a damn cold," she chuckled. "I would never deny the fact that your father loved me, but he didn't love himself. He felt like he needed more to feel complete. I gave that man all of me but, yet, I still wasn't enough in his eyes, so he went out and got more, regardless of him putting that ring on my finger. Now, as far as Harmony goes, her mother and father abandoned her. When raising a child time is the most precious thing to them, understand?"

Chaos wiped his hand down his face as he looked at his mother. He would never forgive Harmony for violating him, but he took just a little bit of responsibility because he was forever busy.

"Mom, I gave this woman the world and, just because I couldn't give her all of my time, she goes out there and cheat?"

"Chaos, it ain't right, but it happens. Harmony was damaged from the jump, and she never got closure. So, whatever demons she had when you met her, she brought that into yawl's marriage. Now, I'm not saying go get back with her because she needs to be taught a lesson, but what I will say is that when it comes to a relationship or marriage. Time is a precious thing and you can't waste it. Choose who to spend your time with wisely and, with her being your wife, and she can't even receive a little bit of your time and attention. What do you think is going to happen? What if the shoe was on the other foot and Harmony was always at the boutique all hours of the night?"

"I understand everything you sayin' ma, but this shit is crazy. I bust my ass to get. Although she don't know what it feels like to grow up strugglin', I still allowed her to enjoy the lavish life. Yea, I spend more time than I should at the club, but I'm making money. I wanna be set for life ma. I don't ever wanna go without again. I swear I don't, and the fact that she don't understand that fucks me up inside," Chaos' voice cracked, but he refused to shed another tear.

"Harmony is wrong, and there is no doubt about it but, baby, you have to understand that money and love go hand and hand sometimes. Sometimes, a man will love his money more than he loves his woman and, sometimes, a woman will love her man more than she loves her money; once again, that was just an example. Your father loved me and he gave me anything I wanted, but what he didn't give me was what I needed. I needed him and all of him. I needed him to be home with his family, instead of running the streets time and time again. What I needed from him didn't matter in his eyes, and that's when I took matters into my own hands. I stepped out on your father," Casey said.

Chaos looked at his mother shockingly. He was unaware that his mother ever stepped out on his father, and he would have never thought that she had something like that in her.

"You serious?" he asked in a surprised tone.

"Yup, as a heart attack. What was supposed to be an innocent date turned into me and him going back to his place and having the most passionate sex ever," Casey explained.

Chaos frowned because he didn't want to hear about his mother getting her boots knocked.

"What you frowning for? How you think you got here? Momma ain't innocent by far when it came to getting hers off," she laughed and continued to fold her clothing. "Anyhow, that man treated my body like the temple it was; he pleased me and gave me all of his time and attention. It brought back memories of how your father made love to me."

Casey got teary-eyed as she revealed her secret to her son. It had been many years since she ever spoke of it, but now was the time to do so.

"Did dad find out?" He was curious to know.

"Yea, he did. You know that saying when you know that you're messing up, but your woman is still walking around the house smiling, it's another man? Although it only happened once, your father saw a drastic change in me. Without me even having to confess what I'd done, he knew. But, then again, that was just the type of man he was; he was wise, and he could figure out stuff without one even having to tell him. Anyway, he asked me was there someone else, and all I did was look at him. I didn't say one word because the many times that I asked him was he cheating, he would always deny it. I didn't lie, but I also didn't give him the truth because I didn't feel as though he deserved it. At the time, I wanted him to wonder about the things I was doing. I wanted him to be in the dark like he had me in the dark. I wanted your father to feel the way he made me feel for many years. It was wrong, but that little bit of get back helped me keep my sanity when the cheating got worse. It helped me get through your father's death. Like I said before, if your father would have stayed home and been faithful to his family, he would still be alive and that's the truth. So, baby, what I'm trying to say is you gotta realize when enough is enough. I'm not telling you to put your job on the back burner, but what I am saying is make time for your wife and for your business. Even it out because a happy wife makes a happy life."

Chaos sat there in silence. In just an hour or so, he had learned so much about his mother, father, marriage, and himself. He appreciated his mother's flaws because it helped him in his current problems. He was still hurting from what Harmony did to him, but he had to admit that he could have done things differently when it came to balancing things out. No matter how right or wrong he was though, he still couldn't find himself getting back with Harmony. That idea was out and it was never going to resurface, no matter how much his mother preached to him.

Chapter Eight

Harmony Winfield-Miller:

Ring. Ring.

Ring.

Harmony had just got finished getting dressed when her cellphone went off. She looked at the number and mixed feelings came over her body. She wanted to be happy, but everything that had been going on caused her to feel under the weather.

"Hello," she answered.

"Hello Mrs. Winfield, this is Rachel. I will be sending you an email of three different designs that Mr. Ford has created. He wants you to look at them and add on your creation, so you both can come up with something fantastic!" Rachel spoke with such excitement.

Harmony gave a dry smile, as if she could be seen. That was music to her ears, but she couldn't celebrate in the state of mind she was in. She tried so hard not to allow herself to fall short like she did the other day but, due to her being pregnant, her emotions were running wild so it was out of her control.

"Oh my, that's wonderful news! I can't wait to see the designs. Is it just clothing or shoes?" she eagerly wanted to know.

"Both! You will be collaborating on both. This is big Mrs. Winfield, so put your all into it because this will hit stores all over the world!" Rachel revealed.

Harmony's palms got sweaty. Hearing that made her nervous and excited, all in one. Love and Harmony's boutique was all over, due to her having an online store as well, but her product wasn't worldwide so she was ecstatic about what was to come.

"This is amazing! Thank you so much, Rachel! I look forward to your email."

"Great! I will be sending it shortly. Have a great day Mrs. Winfield!"

"You too, Rachel!"

Click.

The call ended and Harmony scrolled through her contacts and clicked on Chaos' name. Just as it began to ring, she ended the call.

"Damn, what am I doing?" she asked herself.

She knew that she was the last person that Chaos wanted to hear from, but she couldn't stop herself. Harmony wanted to share that moment with him, but she knew she couldn't. Disappointed in herself, Harmony went into the bathroom to fix her hair. Lost in her own thoughts, she never heard the bedroom door open.

"What the fuck you callin' me for?" Chaos' voice boomed through the silent bedroom.

Harmony jumped when she saw Chaos standing in the doorway of the bathroom. He had a nasty scowl on his face, and she could tell just the sight of her made him upset.

"I-it was by accident," she lied.

"Bullshit. I ain't talk to ya ass in a few days. How the fuck you call me by accident, when I know damn well I wasn't in ya recent calls. The fuck you want?" he asked.

"Nothing, Chaos, damn," she said to him. Harmony didn't want any problems. She had been throwing up all morning, and she had to get to work soon.

"Still lyin' I see. I guess that's just somethin' you good at doin' huh? You just a lyin' piece of shit, to keep it real," Chaos said.

He was still pissed and he wanted Harmony to feel the heat he was carrying. Chaos was intentionally picking a fight because he felt like he had every right to, considering she was the one in the wrong.

"Chaos, stop. I said it was a mistake. No need to get all disrespectful. Don't you think you did enough of that?" she asked.

Chaos frowned his face upon her. "The fuck you mean, don't you know I did enough? Bitch, I ain't did too much of anything, let you tell it. You out here fuckin' and suckin' another nigga, but you mad because I'm disrespectin' you? Be thankful that ya dumb ass is still alive!" he barked.

Harmony was pissing him off, and it took everything in Chaos not to choke the living daylights out of her ass.

"Stop calling me a bitch, Chaos! I am still your wife!"

Harmony was tired of the disrespect. She knew what she did was wrong, but Chaos was acting like he didn't know who she was. The words that were coming out of his mouth was so hurtful and she couldn't stand for it anymore.

"Wife? Nah, you ain't shit to me. You pregnant with another nigga seed and you talkin' about you're still my wife? Get the fuck outta here wit' that shit." He waved her off.

"Fuck you!" Harmony threw the brush down and pushed past Chaos.

He grabbed her arm and pulled her back into the bathroom, slamming her up against the door.

"Don't push it bitch. Because I should've kilt ya ass for the bullshit you did. Choosing another nigga over six fuckin' years? A piece of dick was that important to you? And, on top of that, you couldn't even fuckin' tell me that you weren't happy? You gon' write me a damn letter like a high schooler? The fuck is wrong wit' you, Harmony? We ain't better than that?"

Harmony could hear the hurt and pain in Chaos' voice, causing the tears that she was holding back to run down her face. She never meant to hurt Chaos, but all she wanted was her husband to notice her. She never wanted things between she and Kaotic to go as far as they did, but now there was nothing she could do.

"Chaos, I'm sorry, I really am. It was never supposed to happen like this. I wanted to tell you, but I didn't know how. You were going through your recovery and I just didn't think it was the right time," she explained.

Chaos squinted his eyes and bit his bottom lip. Hearing Harmony speak made him angrier. He grabbed her by the neck and slammed her against the bathroom door once more.

"While I was goin' through recovery?" he asked.

Harmony looked up at him, but she didn't speak.

"Answer me!" he growled.

"Yes," she cried.

Slam!

Slam!

Chaos held her neck with force as he slammed her body up against the door twice. That was all he could do because he couldn't find himself actually causing harm to Harmony, but shaking her ass up was good enough for him.

"You was fuckin' this nigga while I was in the hospital, wasn't you? Tell the fuckin' truth because you ain't just meet this nigga outta nowhere. Tell me the fuckin' truth Harmony! You was fuckin' this nigga while I was on my death bed?"

Harmony cried hard. She never wanted to reveal the cold truth, but she had no choice to. It was too late and no need to hold back any longer.

"Yes Chaos, yes. While you were in the hospital, I slept with him. I'm so sorry baby. I swear I am!" she cried, hoping he would forgive her.

Slam!

Chaos slammed her up against the wall once more before going into the bedroom. He began pacing back and forth as he tried his best not to pull out his gun and empty his clip into Harmony.

"I can't fuckin' believe you yo! You fucked this nigga while I was in the hospital all shot the fuck up, and you bitched and complained about Brittany being there?"

Just by the mention of Brittany's name, Harmony became upset.

"Don't defend that bitch in my house! She still wants to fuck you so, hell yea, I'ma have a problem with her coming up there visiting you. What the fuck do you expect? I am your wife, Chaos!" Harmony screamed.

"I don't wanna hear that shit, and ain't nobody defending that bitch! You was wit' another nigga, when you was supposed to be by my side. You fucked up, not me, so don't try to flip this shit. You got me fucked up right about now. I honestly don't even know why I'm fuckin' talkin' to you. Shit, let me call Brittany because she ain't never turned her back on a nigga," Chaos shot back.

Chaos' words cut deep like a brand-new knife out the box. She couldn't believe that Chaos would go that far to try and break her. Harmony knew the mistake she had made was a bad and unforgiveable one, but she never would have thought that she would ever see this side of Chaos; the side that didn't care about her feelings or care about the way he spoke to her.

"Are you fuckin' serious? You gon' really say that to me, Chaos? So, you fuckin' her? No wonder that bitch popped back up. You wanna get mad at me for sleeping around, but I'm glad I did it. Because you was doing the same thing!"

Chaos stopped in his tracks when Harmony said what she said. He went to reach under his shirt, but he stopped himself. He knew that his words hurt Harmony and she was just clapping back so, instead of trying to harm her physically, which was something he would never do, he decided to continue to break her down with his words.

"Yea, you right. I was fuckin' her, and I still am. Brittany gettin' all this big black dick. Now, you got a reason to be mad. When you think I'm fuckin', understand that I'm fuckin' her," he shot back.

Harmony couldn't control the tears that fell from her eyes. She watched as Chaos got a duffle bag out of the closet and began to pack up some of his belongings.

"Chaos, please, I didn't mean what I said. Baby please, I can't stomach to see any other woman having you. Please don't do this," she pleaded.

Chaos ignored her and threw the duffle bag over his shoulder. He proceeded to walk out the door, but Harmony grabbed him.

"Get the fuck off me!" He looked her up and down with hate in his eyes.

"Please," she said.

"Fuck you and fuck this fake ass marriage. I want a divorce," were the last words he spoke to her before walking out of the bedroom and heading down the stairs.

Bang!

Harmony jumped as the house shook from the force that came from Chaos slamming the door. She dropped down on the floor and cried her eyes out like she never did before.

This is the end. This is truly the end, she thought.

Chapter Nine

Renee & Brave:

Renee was drained when she finally got off work at 4:00 p.m. The boutique had been busy since Harmony reopened it and word got out that Harmony was working with Tom Ford. Customers were swarming in like bees on honey on a sweltering day. She was busy with the customers and trying to keep Harmony from crying all day. After about several attempts, Harmony finally got back on her boss shit and handled her business like she should.

Although she was tired, days like that gave her a rush and the boost she needed. Her income was increasing and her saving skills had gotten much better over the last couple of months. Pretty soon, she was going to buy a car and possibly put a down payment on an affordable but nice house.

Success was eating at Renee's mind, and making sure her kids had everything they needed was the number one factor.

Ring. Ring.

Ring.

Just as the cab pulled up to her apartment, Renee's phone went off. She looked down and saw that it was Brave calling. She rolled her eyes and wondered what he wanted because they hadn't spoken since the argument they had at Harmony's house Saturday.

"Hello?" she answered in an uninterested tone.

"Oh, that's how we answerin' the phone now?" he asked.

"What do you want, Brave?" Renee was in no mood for his bullshit. She had mad love for Brave, but she didn't like how he came at her.

"You got me fucked up, ma. We ain't gon' be talkin' like that, nah. Not to me you not. If I come at you with respect, best believe I want that shit back," he spoke with a firm voice.

"Were you thinkin' about respect when you came at me all fuckin' crazy this past Saturday? Fuck outta here wit' that respect shit Brave!" Renee fumed.

Brave looked at his cellphone with eye brows raised. He even had to chuckle a little at Renee's outburst. Renee had a lot of learning to do, but he respected how she didn't back down from him. She was going to learn that, regardless if they were friends or not, there was only one person that wore the pants, and that was Brave.

He cleared his throat. "Let me ask you somethin' ma."

"What!" Renee asked.

"Real shit ma, who the fuck you think you talkin' to?" Brave didn't wait for a response before he continued. "You think I'm one of them fuck boy ass niggas that you fucked wit' in the past? Huh? Oh, you ain't got shit to say now but, before, you was runnin' ya muthafuckin' mouth like I was some bitch ass nigga. I'ma boss, ma! My whole existence and persona speaks for itself. I shouldn't have to say the shit twice so, after this, I shouldn't have to say it again. Watch ya mouth and ya attitude when you comin' at me, ight?"

Now, it was time for Renee to look at her phone. The way Brave checked her without calling her a bitch or degrading her in any way confused her. She wasn't used to being checked in that manner. Granted, he used profanity, but not once did he disrespect her.

"I hear you. So, anyway. What is it that you want?" Renee couldn't see herself backing all the way down for any man, but she straightened her attitude up.

"Nah, don't hear me. Make sure you listenin'," he said.

"Alright Brave, damn. Can you just tell me what you want because I'm tired?"

Brave lit his blunt, took a couple of pulls, and exhaled the smoke. "You know anything about Harmony fuckin' around on Chaos?" he asked, getting straight to the point.

Renee sighed. She couldn't understand why Brave was asking her a question he asked before. She was going to give him the same answer because her loyalty was with Harmony, regardless of how wrong her friend was.

"I told you before I didn't know anything," she stated.

"Why you lyin' yo?" Brave was not convinced.

He was a street nigga and he knew how females were. He knew that, if Renee didn't know everything, he figured she at least knew about some of it. Brave wanted to get to the bottom of things. It wasn't his business, but Chaos was his bro, and Harmony was his sis. Their love was real and it was strong. Harmony fought tooth and claw to be with Chaos, so Brave couldn't understand why she would go out of her way just to cheat on him.

Harmony was wrong, without a doubt, but Brave knew there was more to the story and what was going on. He figured the least he could do was help Chaos get closure.

"Brave, I'm not lyin' and, if I knew anything, I wouldn't tell you. I'm sure you know things about Chaos that Harmony don't. So, please don't come checkin' me about a situation I have nothing to do with." Renee wasn't the least bit of interested in the current conversation they were having.

"Don't try to flip this shirt. Furthermore, if Chaos did some fucked up shit, I would check him about it and let him know that he was wrong. He would have to go to Harmony himself because that's not my place to relay messages concerning their relationship."

Renee had to laugh at Brave's response. He had just answered his own question.

"My point exactly! You gonna check him in private, right? Then, you just said it's not ya place to get involved in what they got goin' on. So, why do you want me to get in it? This has nothing to do with me nor you, so I'm not sure why you tryna make it seem as if it does have anything to do with us."

"Did I say it had anything to do wit' us? I just know you know somethin', and you gonna tell me sooner or later," Brave spoke with confidence.

Renee sighed loudly. "I'ma talk to you later, Brave. I just got off work and I'm tired. I don't have time for this right now," Renee attempted to end the call.

"Don't play wit' me, yo. I swear you testin' my patience right now," Brave told her.

"I'm not testing anything but, like I said before, I'm tired. We can talk later, ight?" Renee said.

"Oh, I see what type of time you on, cool."

Click.

Renee looked at the phone and shook her head. If she wasn't so tired, she would have called his ass back and cursed him the fuck out, but she let it slide for now. She took her keys out her purse, unlocked the door, and walked in, closing it behind her. The kids were still at the babysitter's, and she took this time to take a quick power nap before having to pick them up tonight.

She headed straight down the mini hallway to the living room, dropped her purse on the table, kicked off her shoes, and laid down on the couch. The soft pillows felt so good to her body as it sunk in the texture. Renee wasted no time getting comfortable and falling asleep.

***

Harmony Winfield-Miller:

After having a long day and even longer morning, Harmony was finally wrapping things up at the boutique. Her attitude had gotten much better once Renee whipped her into shape, on top of her receiving the emails of the designs Tom Ford came up with from Rachel. Despite how bad things were in her personal life, Harmony could still see God's work and she was more than thankful for the blessings that was raining upon her.

It was going on 5:45 p.m. and her boutique was just minutes away from closing when she heard the *ding* sound, letting her know that someone had entered her store. The last of her new employees had gotten off at 5:30 p.m., so she took a glance at the security camera to see who was walking in. She expected it to be a customer trying to purchase an item before they closed, but what she saw on the security camera made her attitude come back within a split second.

Harmony hopped up out of her swivel chair and speed walked around her desk and to the door. She slung her office door open and walked out with one hand on her hip.

"What the fuck are you doing here Kaotic? Get the fuck out before I call the cops on ya dumb ass!" she snapped.

Kaotic laughed at her anger. He wasn't fazed at all by her outburst. "Calm down wit' all that bullshit you spittin'. You act like you ain't miss a nigga," he told her.

"Are you fuckin' stupid? I don't miss you, nor do I want ya dirty ass! Get the fuck outta here! I swear, that's gonna be my last time tellin' you!"

"Bitch, stop lyin' to yaself. You know you miss the hell outta me. I bet you miss me diggin' them guts out, don't you? Havin' this dick all up in that pussy and watchin' you cream on it. You miss that shit, right?" Kaotic taunted.

"Nigga, you think I'm playin'," Harmony said as she turned around and headed back to her office.

She didn't know that Kaotic was right on her heels. The moment she tried to reach over her desk to grab her cellphone, Kaotic grabbed a handful of her hair and yanked her head back, spinning her around. With quick speed, his hand was around her neck.

"Bitch, don't fuckin' play wit' me. Who you think you fuckin' wit'?" he barked.

Harmony was shocked by him manhandling her. "Are fuck you fuckin' stupid? My husband will kill you. Get your fuckin' hands off me!" she gasped for air.

Kaotic laughed loud and hard. "Bitch, Chaos don't fuck wit' you. I'm sure the text I sent him stopped all that shit. Then, on top of that, you done told the nigga everything. You fucked baby girl," he bragged.

This was the second time Harmony heard about pictures being sent. She wondered what Brave and, now, Kaotic was talking about because from what she knew, she never took any pictures with Kaotic.

"What pictures are you talking about?" she asked, still trying to loosen his grip on her neck.

Kaotic smirked and pulled out his cellphone while his hand was still gripped around her neck, tight enough for her to know that he was not bullshitting. Harmony watched as he scrolled and swiped through his phone. Before she knew it, he turned the phone around and held it up to her face so that she could see her nude photos he'd snuck and took while she was asleep.

"This all you, ma, all you."

Kaotic swiped left a few times, so she could see each picture he took. Harmony was embarrassed, and she couldn't blame Chaos for being so angry. She never knew that Kaotic had done such thing while she was sleeping, but as the saying goes: if you lay down with dogs, you're bound to get up with fleas.

"You dirty bastard!" she screamed. The warm tears welled up in her eyes and flowed down her cheeks like a waterfall. Her outburst only made Kaotic laugh, and it fed his ego.

"I gotta agree wit' you there. I heard my pops died. Damn, at least Chaos got a chance to spend time wit' him before he did."

Harmony finally had enough of Kaotic's antics and secrets.

Slap!

"You fuckin' crazy ass bitch!" Kaotic winced as he held his face.

Harmony had completely caught Kaotic off guard when she slapped him across his face. She didn't give a fuck because after that, he knew to remove his damn hand from around her neck.

"You damn right nigga! You have caused nothing but trouble since you entered my life, and now you wanna walk ya dusty ass up to my place of business and start some more shit? What the fuck is your problem? And what right do you have to mention my husband's late father?"

"You funny as fuck. You caused ya own damn problems, you unsatisfied, whore ass bitch. The fuck you thought, this shit was just a coincidence? The moment you gave me ya time, I knew that I had you.

Not to mention, my brother ain't do what he was supposed to do when it came to you, so it was more than easy enough for me to get in," Kaotic explained.

"Nigga, fuck outta here! I didn't give you any of my time! And what the fuck you mean brother? Don't fuckin' play with me! I am not in the mood," Harmony spat.

The truth was right there in Harmony's face, but she kept on blocking it out. She didn't want to believe that she had been sleeping with her husband's brother.

"You stupid as hell if you ain't caught on by now," Kaotic shot back.

Harmony's nostrils flared as she quickly thought about the day she and Kaotic first met.

"Good morning, beautiful." He showed his pearly whites.

Harmony had just opened her car door, but stopped to see who was talking to her. The guy didn't look familiar to her and she intended to just get in her car and pull off, but she didn't want to be rude.

"Good morning, sir," she responded as she got in her car.

Kaotic walked to the driver's side and stood there until she rolled the window down.

"Can I help you with something?" she asked.

"You can start by giving me your number gorgeous," he said.

Harmony waved him off. "Sorry, but I'm married."

Kaotic couldn't give two fucks if Jesus was her husband. He wanted her number and, regardless if she liked it or not, he was damn sure going to get it.

"Check this. I'm well aware of that nigga Chaos bein' ya husband but, in all honesty baby, he's the least of my worries. I'm tryna get to know you as a friend. I wouldn't mind taking you out to eat and having some good ass conversation; now, like I said, you can start by giving me your number."

Harmony was taken aback by his forwardness. She couldn't believe how turned on she was by the man that stood before her. Although her and Chaos made up, she still was a little bothered by the stunt he pulled on Sunday.

"I like your mentality, but that don't mean I'ma give you my number. I'm very faithful to my husband and I'll be damned if I let six years go down the drain just because you're interested in me," she said with much attitude.

Kaotic laughed because she fucked up and let him in, and she didn't even know it. Just by her keeping up the conversation let him know that she was interested in him and willing to take things further, if the opportunity presented itself.

"Sssss, feisty, I like that. You tryna play hard to get, and shit like that get a nigga dick hard." He reached her car window, grabbed her hand, and placed it on his bulge.

Harmony felt his thickness and her pussy got wet. She quickly snatched her hand away and started up her car.

"I gotta go because you trippin' nigga."

"You ain't going nowhere until you pass off them digits," he stated.

Harmony bit her bottom lip and thought on it for a moment. The brother was fine as wine, and his muscles were busting through his white t-shirt. There wasn't another man that ever caught her eye until now.

A friend won't hurt, she thought.

"Fine, my number is..."

Kaotic stored her number, stuck his head in her window, and kissed her on the lips. Harmony was caught completely off guard but, once she felt the softness of his lips, she didn't deny him the kiss.

"Believe me, baby, there's plenty more where that came from," Kaotic said as he walked away, leaving Harmony in a trance.

She couldn't believe how she just disrespected Chao behind his back. That was something she never done before and she was disappointed in herself for doing it. It was as if it turned her on for doing the wrong things.

Harmony didn't think she could cry anymore, but she did. The more she thought about when she and Kaotic first met, she realized that she gave him too much of her time and attention from jump. She should have never entertained him the way that she did, and that was where she fucked up at.

"I fucked up by letting a piece of shit like you come between me and my marriage. I don't know what I was thinking, but my husband was all the man I needed then and now," she said through a cracked voice.

"Yea, well, I ain't hear none of that bullshit when I had my dick deep in ya stomach, now did I?" he asked and then did the birdman hand rub. "Now, back to the situation at hand."

"Get the fuck out!" Harmony became furious.

She didn't want to have any further conversation with him, especially knowing that the security cameras were still on and Chaos had access to them, regardless if it was her boutique or not. Harmony didn't want anything else jeopardizing what she was trying hard to fix.

"I'm not goin' anywhere and, oh, to answer ya question. What do I mean about brother? Hence, the similarity in our names jackass," Kaotic said to her.

Harmony shook her head no. "Impossible. Chaos doesn't have any siblings," she said as she continuously shook her head.

"Yea, that's what Casey snake ass want yawl to think. I'm his brother, bitch. Kaotic muthafuckin' Miller in the fuckin' flesh. We fraternal twins, share the same blood."

Just then, Harmony got dizzy. She held onto the desk as she slowly walked around to the other side to take a seat.

"This can't be true. It just can't be. I might be pregnant by my husband's brother?" Harmony was thinking out loud.

Kaotic looked at her suspiciously. "The fuck you mean, pregnant?" he asked.

"Don't worry about it! Just please get the fuck out!" Harmony was overwhelmed.

Kaotic shook his head back and forth. "Damn ma. You caught up in more bullshit then a little bit. I would hate for Chaos to find out that I was the one who let that clip go the night he got shot. What's even more fucked up is the fact that you, my friend, was fuckin' the nigga who tried to take his life," Kaotic laughed. "You ain't never gettin' that nigga back. You can forget that."

He finally turned and walked out of Harmony's office and then left the boutique after he dropped the bomb on her. Harmony, on the other hand, was an emotional wreck. She cried hysterically, trying to take everything in that was just told to her. She couldn't blame Chaos for looking at her like she was a fucked-up person because this was a fucked-up situation.

There was no way she could tell Chaos that Kaotic was his brother, she was fucking him, and he was the one that tried to kill him. Harmony was in a lose-lose situation, and she didn't know which way to turn on how to get out of this mess she caused on herself.

Chapter Ten

Brave & Renee:

It was 11:45 p.m. later that Monday evening when Brave pulled up to Renee's apartment and parked. The projects was still lit around that time. He sat in his 2016 all-black Cadillac Escalade while finishing off the last of his blunt. Brave could sense that all eyes were on him, but he was waiting for a nigga to pop stupid, so he could let one off.

Brave had just gotten off work, and he was tired. He was not for any bullshit at all. Tonight was one of the first nights since Centerfolds had been open that Chaos closed early. They usually closed in the wee hours of the morning but, for some reason, Brave noticed a slight change in Chaos since he and Harmony hadn't been together.

Beep!
Beep!

Brave finally got out of his truck and locked the doors. He dusted off his clothes to make sure he was good before walking up to Renee's door.

Knock. Knock.

Knock.

Brave heard whispers as he waited for Renee to answer the door. It was late, so he assumed she was sleeping, but he wanted to surprise her, considering they hadn't been on the best of terms since Harmony and Chaos had been going through their little dispute. Brave was feeling Renee, but he most definitely didn't want to move too fast because he wasn't the relationship type. Then, after seeing what Chaos was going through, he couldn't find himself in a situation like that because he would dead a bitch without hesitation.

Knock. Knock.

Knock.

"Yo, wassup? You must got the wrong apartment number or somethin' because that's my homeboy BM crib, and I know he ain't allowin' no otha nigga to take care of what he pay for." A tall, slinky, dark skinned dude attempted to walk up on Brave.

He had a few young boys following him but, the moment Brave pulled out his 40. Caliber, the young boys quickly backed up, but the tall, slinky guy seemed to have heart.

"Nigga, you must wanna die tonight?" Brave asked.

"Shit, I'm wonderin' the same thing about you. Because once my homeboy finds out about this shit here. Shit gon' get hella real," he bragged.

Click.

Clack.

Brave cocked his burner back and walked closer to the guy. He didn't give a fuck about who saw him; when it came to disrespect, it was bound to get ugly. He was tired and he was in no mood for the bullshit.

"Brave!" Renee yelled when she saw what was about to transpire in front of her.

He didn't even hear the door open, but he snapped back into reality when she started tugging on his arm.

"What the hell is going on?" she asked.

"I'm about to buss a nigga head, that's what the fuck is goin' on."

Brave normally didn't explain himself when it came to a situation like the one he was in but, for some reason, he felt the need to hold off on dude. Not because of what he said, but because the sound of Renee's voice put him at ease.

"Brave, this bum ass nigga ain't worth it. Come in the house right now," she said in a firm voice.

"Renee, you fuckin' this nigga?" the tall, slinky guy asked.

Renee looked at him in disgust. It was dark outside, but the glow from the street lights and the outside lights from the apartments allowed the guy to see how disgusted Renee truly was.

"Don't worry about if I'm fuckin' him or not. I'ma grown ass woman, and you can tell ya deadbeat ass homeboy whatever the fuck you want. That nigga been dead to me, and ya best bet is to leave well enough alone before you become a dead nigga fareal!" she snapped.

Brave cocked his head to the side and squinted his eyes. He waited for the nigga who stood before him to make a move. The guy put his hands up and nodded his head up and down before slowly walking backwards.

"A'ight, you got it. But, when Bud hear about this, you know shit gon' get real," he promised.

"Tell ya homeboy to buss a move bitch!" Brave shot back.

Renee grabbed Brave by the arm and pulled him into the apartment. She slammed the door shut and looked at him with a confused looked.

"What are you doing here? And what the hell happened out there?" She wanted to know.

"I wanted to come by to check you since I got off work early, but that nigga out there wanted problems and he almost got em if you didn't come out there playin' super save a nigga," he explained.

"What the fuck is that supposed to mean?" she asked while placing both hands on her hips.

"You still fuckin' ya baby dad? Because you def' don't need to be checkin' for a nigga like me if you dealin' wit' bum ass niggas that can't even take care of they kids."

Renee's mouth fell wide open.

"Who the fuck do you think you talkin' to like that? Don't come to my muthafuckin' place talkin' down on me. I ain't fuckin' with nobody! And if I was, that's my muthafuckin' business nigga! You don't pay shit up in here, I do! I bust my ass all day every fuckin' day to make sure my bills is paid and my kids is fed. So, what? You want that gas money or babysitter money you gave me, is that it? Because I'll go broke before I let any nigga throw some chump change ass shit up in my face!"

Renee was fuming. She couldn't believe Brave had the nerve to come at her the way he was coming. Not once did she come at him about who he could have been fucking.

"You poppin' off like this nigga ain't just come at me all crazy because I was knockin' on ya door. Why the fuck would ya baby dad give a fuck about what nigga in ya house if yawl still ain't fuckin'? Then, you talkin' about you pay the bills but, from what that nigga was sayin', you don't pay shit," Brave shot back.

He was testing Renee to see how honest she would be with him. He knew the nigga outside was lying, but he wanted to continue to see what Renee was really about before he continued to make moves with her and on her. Brave couldn't give two fucks to what the dude outside was saying, but he didn't like being disrespected, nor did he appreciate being threatened over some baby daddy shit that he had nothing to do with.

"Ain't nobody fuckin' that dusty ass nigga! I take care of my kids! All three of them, and I've been doing it by my damn self for years. Even when me and that bum ass nigga was together, I was still a single damn parent. If that nigga wasn't beating my ass, he was taking from me and my kids to support his bum ass drinking habit. I bust my ass at *Love and Harmony* every day, sometimes on my days off, just to make sure my check is fat. I even do hair on the side to have a few extra dollars. I don't even know why I'm explaining shit to you because you ain't my fucking nigga, but don't you ever come at me like I don't hold my own."

Brave checked Renee out from head to toe before pushing past her. He looked to his left and saw the kitchen, but kept straight until he got to the living room. He saw a young boy sleeping on the couch, which he assumed was one of her children that she told him about.

"Homie must sleep hard as fuck. All that damn yellin' you was doin'," Brave said in a low tone.

Renee had a stank face on. The fact that Brave got her all riled up just to act as calm as ever bothered the fuck out of her.

"Are you fuckin' serious?" she asked with her arms folded across her chest as she walked down the hallway and into the living room.

"Shhh." Brave put his finger to his mouth. "You loud as fuck."

He then left out of the living room and past the bathroom on the left, a bedroom, and a closet, which he assumed was on the right. When he saw the last door open at the end of the hall, he knew that was Renee's room and he welcomed himself to it.

"What are you doing?" she whispered as she followed him.

Brave paid her no mind. He walked into her bedroom and the sweet smell of Vanilla hit his nose. He saw candles burning and he instantly knew that he was about to get some good relaxation going on. He kicked off his sneakers, took off his deep, dark blue denim jeans, and t-shirt, which left him in a white beater tank top and boxer briefs.

Renee watched him sit on her bed, lie back, and get comfortable. She couldn't believe how at home he was because of the type of man she assumed he was. Never would she have thought that Brave would step foot in her apartment, let alone in her bedroom and be as comfortable as he was at that moment.

"What?" he asked, as he placed his hand in the back of his head.

"You just gonna start all that shit and then hop ya yellow ass in my bed?"

Brave partially sat up, leaned over, and reached into his jean pocket to grab his lighter. He then sparked up the other blunt he rolled before leaving the club. He lit up his blunt and took a couple of pulls.

Cough! Cough!

Cough!

Brave looked Renee up and down and he was more than attracted to her. She looked like a freshly unwrapped Hershey's Kiss candy. She was five-foot-one-inches, and her measurements were 34-27-32 and she was a solid one hundred and seventy pounds. He wanted to fuck Renee something serious but, when they first met, he had to feel her out. There was still more to learn about her and her to learn about him, but he didn't mind taking the next step and seeing how she felt inside.

"You gon' stand there or get in the bed?"

Renee was at a loss for words. Everything Brave was doing was mind boggling to her. She didn't want to get ahead of herself and he come out and say he was joking but, then again, she remembered what Harmony said about him being a real stand up ass nigga, so what was transpiring at that moment was nothing more than the real thing, and she knew she had to take advantage of it. However, the moment she walked around to the other side of the bed, pulled the covers back, and climbed in, she bitched out.

The smell of Brave's cologne had her kitty cat running wild.

Get a hold of yaself bitch! her inner self spoke to her.

Renee took a deep breath to try and hold her composure because her pussy was on fire for Brave. Brave, on the other hand, laughed inside as he took pull after pull of his blunt because he knew Renee wanted him. He didn't expect her to make the first move because he wasn't that type of nigga. If he wanted you, he damn sure was going to make it obvious.

"You gotta nice lil spot," Brave said while breaking the awkward silence.

"You think so?" she asked, as if what he said was weird.

Brave glanced over at her. "Yea. Why you say it like that?"

"I mean, just by the way I thought you were. I didn't think you would even acknowledge me or even come chill with me the way you doing."

Brave frowned his face up and looked over at her. "The fuck you mean? We chilled before. You done sat on my damn bed before ma. What the fuck you talkin' about?"

"Brave, you know what I'm saying. I live in the projects. You live in a damn one-story house. Like, granted, we chilled before, you done drove me around in ya truck, but to actually pop up, come in my house, and get in my bed. That's some new shit coming from you."

Brave looked around for an ashtray, but soon realized he wasn't going to find one because Renee didn't smoke. He took it upon himself to get up and leave out of the bedroom, heading down the hall and into the bathroom to run a little water over the tip of the blunt to put it out. Once he was done, he walked back down the hall and into the bedroom, closing the door behind him and locking it.

"What are you doing?" she asked, confused once again.

Brave waved her off. He put his piece of blunt on the mini nightstand beside Renee's bed and then got back on the bed and under the covers.

"Remember when I said you say the wrong shit at the wrong fuckin' time? If I didn't wanna see what you was about, I would've turned the other cheek when I first saw you that night at the club. I can tell just by the way you look that you a hood chick, but I looked past that. We exchanged numbers and, now, we here. Don't fuck it up because you just seconds away from doing so," Brave explained.

Renee was quiet for a brief second. She didn't want to mess things up with Brave because things were going smooth, despite the little mishap they had due to Harmony and Chaos' beef. Other than that, they were building a solid friendship and she was enjoying it because that was something she'd never done before.

"That ain't even what type of time I'm on. I'm just saying what it is and how I felt. You come off as a nigga that don't fuck with hood bitches or bitches that got darker skin than him. Believe me, I done been through it all, which is why I got tired and left my ugly ass, no-good ass baby daddy."

Brave could sense a lot of hurt and hatred in Renee's voice. If this was any other day or maybe even the first time they had chilled, he would have cursed Renee the fuck out because the shit she was saying was completely blowing his high. But, instead of getting upset, he took it upon himself to try and understand her.

He wasn't the type of nigga that really gave a fuck but, when he cared about you, he would go over and beyond to make sure you was good.

"Why the fuck would you say some shit like that?" he asked.

"Because it's reality, Brave. No matter how much you try to act as if it's not, it is. You a pretty boy, and I'm what they call a ghetto, hood rat ass bitch. You like those pretty model type, light-skinned ass females and that's just that. How many niggas you see walking around with a darker female? A good two percent out of ninety-eight. That's why I look up to Harmony so much, and I'm upset that she fucked up. She's a beautiful chocolate woman who gets respect, and that's something I yearn for."

Brave usually had a response for everything, but this was one time he didn't. He couldn't even get mad at Renee because most of the niggas he knew from back then and now always wanted a light skinned chick with a flat stomach and big ass. He truly didn't understand because at the end of the day, they were all black, but he realized a long time ago that black men were the cause of separating black women, not respecting them, and making them think one skin complexion was better than the next.

"Come here," he told her.

"For what?" Renee looked at Brave confused.

Brave wiped his hand down his face and sighed loudly before rolling over to where Renee was and climbing on top of her. He gently tapped her on her thigh with his right hand so that she could open her legs for him to get between them.

"Wha..."

"Shhh, you talk too much," Brave said before silencing her with a kiss.

He continued by giving her sweet kisses and nibbles on her neck as he rubbed on her thighs. Renee didn't even see Brave's dick yet, but she could feel it growing as it got hard. Just by the feeling, she knew it had a nice thickness to it, and she wasn't quite sure if she was ready to take on all that Brave had to offer. Her pussy was soaked, and all Brave did was give a simple kiss, but the softness of his lips gave her chills all over her body.

"I can't do this shit," Renee managed to get out as she attempted to push Brave away.

She knew them having sex would make the feelings she already had for him run wild twice as bad and she just didn't want to go there with him. Yeah, they would chill together, but she didn't feel like they were ready to do what was about to go down.

Brave ignored Renee and took it upon himself to slide her panties off.

"Come on. Take all this off," he demanded so firm, but yet so smooth.

Renee took a deep breath as she sat up and took off the black t-shirt gown she had on. She threw it on the floor and laid back down. Brave shocked her by pulling her legs down and lifting them up in the air.

"Oh, my God!" she squealed.

Brave went down and began to flick his tongue back and forth, up and down, and around her clit. Renee's pussy was already gushing, and he didn't make it any better when he started fingering her as he slurped on her love cave.

"Ooooo, myyyyy Gggod."

Brave's tongue was magical, the way he took his finger out and made his tongue disappear as he dipped it in and out of her pussy. She knew she had to stop him. Renee couldn't handle what was being given. She had to switch the situation quickly. She gently pushed his head, sat up, and gave him a deep kiss, enough to distract him and switch roles. Renee kissed him steady and, by this time, Brave was on his back; then, she worked her way down. Grabbing his dick, she could feel his hand grip the back of her neck and that turned her on even more. She slobbed him deeply and cupped his balls while he applied pressure to the back of her neck but, just like Renee, Brave knew he had to change the situation.

"Damn, baby, let me taste these lips again," Brave spoke with so much demand, but with a passionate tone.

Renee knew she was getting to him. She got up and allowed Brave to taste her lips. The sweet juices ran down her thighs and she was ready; before he could make a move, she straddled his dick. Brave grabbed her hips and bit his bottom lip.

"Grip that shit," Brave whispered, and that's exactly what Renee did. She arched her back as she rode him steadily, as she tried her best to not concentrate on the pain.

Brave never fucked any female raw, but there was just something special about Renee and he planned on making it official between the two once he helped Chaos with his complicated relationship. He wasn't putting a hold on his love life for Chaos, but he just couldn't find himself gloating his relationship with Renee, when Chaos was going through a tough time with the love of his life.

"Sssss," he sucked his teeth.

As Brave's toes began to curl, he focused himself and rolled her over with his dick still inside her. He began to thrust her pussy with a slight hint of force.

"Oooh, ahhh." Renee took her hand and pushed Brave back a little. She hadn't had sex in over a year and a half, and there was nothing little about the length and width of Brave's dick.

"Don't be scared, put them legs around me," Brave said.

Renee did as she was told and wrapped her legs around his waist, as he deep stroked her. Renee couldn't stop shaking; back to back, she kept cumin'.

"What's ma name?"

"Brave!"

"What Brave doin'?"

Renee didn't answer. She couldn't speak, due to the good dick down she was getting. It had been so long since she had been sexed good, and Brave made the wait well worth it.

"I'm cu—cu—cumin'!" she stuttered as she shook violently.

"Yea, coat that dick wit' all that juice baby."

Renee couldn't stop cumin' if she tried. It was as if Brave was trying to drain everything out of her because he went from deep stroking her with a hint of force, to deep stroking her fast and hard. The bed was shaking and the walls seemed to rattle, as he tore

Renee's pussy up. Their skin was smacking up against one another, and his balls clapped against her ass with each stroke.

Brave applied all his weight onto Renee, as he reached under her and cupped her ass and put every inch of dick he had in her.

"Oh, my God, Brave!"

Brave was face to face with her, but his eyes were closed. "Mmmm."

Renee heard Brave moan as she felt a warm sensation enter her. She could tell that Brave hadn't fucked in a while because he filled her up with his warm semen. It oozed out of her pussy and she could feel it drip between her ass cheeks. Brave opened his eyes and gave Renee a sloppy kiss before removing his hands from underneath her and rolling over.

Renee couldn't move; she was weak, so she just laid on her back and daydreamed about the first day she'd met Brave.

Brave nodded, turned his attention to Renee, and extended his hand. "Wassup gorgeous?"

Renee blushed instantly. All she could do was smile bashfully and sip her drink. She completely ignored the fact that Brave had his hand out.

Harmony chuckled at how nervous Renee got when Brave gave her his attention.

This was nothing new to Brave because he always had the females feeling some kind of way when it came to him. He could literally talk the panties off any woman he wanted. Brave stood directly in front of Renee and leaned over so that both his hands were on the bar and he was face to face with her.

Renee got hot all over and melted inside as she tried to keep her composure. The look Brave was giving her made her want to fuck him right then and there.

"So, you just gon' ignore a nigga?"

Harmony smirked and shook her head. She knew that Brave knew that Renee was feeling him. He was messing with her head at the moment, and Harmony could just imagine how wet Renee's panties were because she could remember a time when Chaos did her the same way.

"Uh, I mean, no," she fumbled to find the words to say.

"That's what it seems like. I done tried to shake ya hand and introduce myself, and you actin' all shy. I don't bite beautiful," he laughed. "I mean, that's only if you want me to."

It was like love at first sight with Renee, and that was a feeling she never felt before. As many times as she fucked her baby dad, not once did she ever have the feeling that Brave was giving her, and the crazy part about it was that he never even touched her. His scent alone had her mind blown.

Brave licked his pink lips. "So, wassup? You gon' tell me ya name?"

Renee took a sip of her drink and looked Brave up and down. His crinkly dreads hung past his shoulders, and she could tell he had just got finished smoking because his eyes were low and she could smell a strong hint of weed that had stayed on his clothes. But, that still didn't take away of the divine smell that came from him.

"It's Renee," she finally spoke up.

Brave stood up and pulled out his phone, while Renee undressed him with her eyes. He was five-foot-eleven, and he had the skin complexion of a cashew peanut. Her eyes couldn't help but to wander downwards and her heart fluttered by the *sight of the huge bulge that could be seen through his jeans.*

"Chill lil mama. This ain't what you want," he said, noticing where her eyes were looking."

Renee quickly looked away embarrassed by being caught acting like a pervert.

"You gon' let a nigga get ya number?"

Renee looked over at Harmony, and Harmony looked back at her with a confused look. "Girl, you better stop playin' and give my bro ya number."

She took another look at Brave and then gave him her number; she watched as he programmed it in his phone.

"A'ight sis. I'm bouta get back here and finish handling business."

When she came back to, all she could do was smile and melt inside. Brave had just come back in the room with a wet washcloth. She didn't mind him cleaning himself off because they both made a mess.

"Here." Brave tried to help clean Renee off.

"I got it. Lay down and get some rest," she said.

Brave chuckled, but he didn't decline the offer to lie down because he was tired. Renee, on the other hand, was still lying on her back while trying to wipe off, but she soon gave up and threw the washcloth on the floor. She smiled inside because the feelings that she had been keeping bottled up for Brave were flowing through her pores at that moment. As she closed her eyes, she prayed that this wasn't the end and that she and Brave would soon be more than friends. She wasn't going to take their sexual encounter and run with it because she knew how guys could be, but she hoped that this time would be different.

"Only time will tell," she whispered, as she looked at Brave before snuggling up against him and drifting off to sleep.

***

Chaos Miller:

Ring. Ring.
Ring.

Chaos had just gotten out of the shower when his phone rang. He was in no mood to talk to anyone but, when he glanced at the screen and saw that it was Brittany calling, he decided to answer to see what it was that she wanted.

"Wassup?" he answered.

"Hey, are you busy?" she asked.

Chaos sighed and looked at the time. "What do you want, Brittany? Its 1 a.m. in the morning and you askin' if I'm busy."

"I miss you. I've been driving past your mother's house and I've been seeing your car. Can I come over and talk?" she asked.

Chaos frowned when he heard Brittany say what she said. She'd always been the stalker type of female, and that was one of the main reasons he left her alone in the past because her clinginess was possessive.

"Brittany, don't start this shit. Why the fuck is you drivin' past my mother's house? This that shit I wasn't feelin' before. If you came by here, then I know for a fact you drove past my house. You crossin' the line once again," Chaos snapped at her.

Brittany smacked her lips. "Well, if you answered ya fuckin' phone, I wouldn't need to drive past your bitch house or ya mom's house!"

Chaos clenched his jaws as he gritted his teeth. "Watch ya fuckin' mouth when you speakin' about my fuckin' wife, bitch. That's what you called for? To talk slick about Harmony?" he asked.

Although Harmony and Chaos weren't together, Chaos wasn't going to allow any female to disrespect her, regardless of who they were and what history they had; she was still his wife.

"No! I called to see if I can come over and talk Chaos. I said I missed you!" she screamed into the phone.

"Miss what?" he asked in confusion.

They had dealt with one another in years. Back when Chaos was in his early to his mid-twenties, he fucked around with Brittany. That was over several years ago, and she still couldn't let the past go.

"Us! I miss what we use to have. It ain't too late to make it work," she said to him.

"Make what work? Brittany, I'm married. Regardless of what you may think, I love my wife. The most I can give you is friendship. Nothing more, but it could be less."

Brittany winced when he spoke about how he loved Harmony. She just couldn't understand why Chaos could leave her high and dry the way he did, in her eyes.

"What is it about her, Chaos? I've played the back seat for the last six years! You act like I didn't hold you down at one point!"

Chaos sighed in frustration.

"I fucked around wit' you the first year me and Harmony started dealing, so don't say you played the back seat for the last six years as if I cheated on Harmony wit' you. Yea, you held me down, but you act like I was the only nigga you was fuckin'?" Chaos shot back.

"Go to hell Chaos because you know my son is yours! You've been treating me like shit since you found out I was pregnant!"

"Fuck outta here wit' that shit girl. How the fuck is that boy mines, when he's three years fuckin' old? The last time I fucked you was over five years ago; you do the fuckin' math! Don't start no dumb shit wit' me. I told you I'll help take care of him, considering I was the only decent male figure in his life, and a lot of that money was to keep you out of my fuckin' life and relationship because I know how the hell you are!"

Chaos was reading Brittany her rights. She had caught him at a bad time and he let her have it from head to toe.

"What the fuck ever Chaos," Brittany responded.

There was nothing else she could say because Chaos was right, but she would never admit that to him or anyone else.

"Yea, whatever, but I don't have time for this. I'm tired and aggravated, so you gon' have to hit me up another time," he told her.

"Chaos, wait!" Brittany stopped him.

"Whatttt Brittany?" he answered in an aggravated tone.

"Can we at least go out for a drink? Dinner? A movie? I'll accept anything Chaos. I've been going through a lot and, right now, I just need a friend," her voice cracked as she spoke.

Chaos shook his head and cursed himself for even answering the phone. He wanted to deny her and hang up the phone, but that just wasn't the type of man he was.

"A'ight, just hit me up and let me know when. I'll let you know if I'm free or not."

That was music to her ears. "Great! That's all I needed to know. We'll be talking soon. Goodnight baby."

Click.

Brittany hung up so fast, Chaos couldn't even respond to her. He shook his head and threw it back on the bed. He didn't even feel like getting dressed anymore, so he pulled the covers back and got under them with his towel still wrapped around his waist. He adjusted the pillow behind his head, placed his right hand behind his head and his left hand inside of the towel, and closed his eyes. Not only was Chaos physically drained, he was also emotionally and mentally drained from life itself.

Chapter Eleven

Brave & Renee:

Renee cracked open her eyes and heard silence. That wasn't normal, considering her kids were always up making noise, regardless of their ages. She reached over and grabbed her cellphone off the nightstand. Once she had it in her hand, she checked the time and it was going on 1:45 p.m.

"Shit!" she spat, as she jumped out of bed.

Renee tripped over the blanket and quickly ran to her closet. She pulled out a colorful stripped sundress and a pair of black sandals that she'd purchased from Walmart. Although Renee had gotten a raise and started to manage her money right, she still didn't buy expensive clothing or shoes. Her dedication was her children, their futures, her home, and her bills.

Once she had gotten out her outfit, she threw it on the bed and went back around the other side of the bed that she slept on to grab her nightgown that she wore the other night.

"That no good bastard!" Renee spat as she put on her night gown. "He could've at least woke me up for work. Just like the rest of these niggas."

Renee left out of the bedroom and headed into the bathroom to turn the shower on before checking on the kids. She checked in the two youngest rooms and they weren't there, so she made her way down the hallway to the living room where her oldest slept. He wasn't on the couch and her apartment wasn't but so big, so she walked down the other hallway and turned to the right to go into the kitchen. She stopped in her tracks when she saw her kids and Brave putting up groceries.

"Mommie! We're having tacos for dinner!" her six-year-old, Re'Niya, squealed.

"Yea, mom, Brave took us all out to get breakfast, and he even brought you something back. We went to pick up a few things from the store after that, and he said he's making us tacos," her oldest, whose name was Raymond, explained to her.

Renee's mouth fell wide open. She didn't know what to say or even how to react. When she didn't see Brave in the bedroom, she immediately thought that he had treated her like her past flings and even her baby daddy.

"That's all very nice," Renee managed to say.

Brave bit his bottom lip and winked at her, which caused Renee to blush.

"You know you wastin' water, right?" he said to her.

"Oh, damn! I'm late for work yawl. Raymond, call the babysitter and let her know yawl will be over today. I'm just running a little late," she explained as she proceeded to turn around.

"Nah, I handled all that already. You off today, I called Harmony already. All you gotta do is call the babysitter and let her know she got the day off," Brave chimed in.

"You did what?" she asked.

"I told Harmony to give you the day off, and I called Chaos to let him know I'll be taking the day off. Don't trip; let's just kick back and relax today wit' the kids," he assured her.

Renee was at a loss for words. From what she understood, Brave didn't even like women with kids, so she was completely taken back by his kind gestures. She didn't want him to feel bad for their lack of a father figure, so she took it upon herself to speak up.

"Brave, can you come to the back with me for a second?" she asked.

Renee headed out of the kitchen and made her way into the bathroom while Brave followed.

"Wassup?" he asked.

"You know you don't have to do this. I know you don't fuck with women that have kids, especially my football team as you call it. So, you don't have to stick around just because you fucked me," Renee said without holding back how she felt.

Brave had his hand in his pocket as he leaned back on the bathroom door. Renee was very attractive to him and she was a decent girl, just a little rough around the edges but, when she spoke, she aggravated the fuck out of Brave and he never hesitated when it came to telling her.

"There you go again," he said as he shook his head. "Sayin' the wrong damn thing at the wrong damn time."

"What was wrong about what I said? I speak my damn mind and, if that's a problem, then we ain't gonna work."

"Speakin' ya mind ma ain't the problem. It's the shit that you be thinkin' about. You a negative ass person and, yea, I know I said what the fuck I said, but what the fuck does that have to do wit' what we got goin' on right now? If I'm rockin' wit' you, let me rock. Don't keep sayin' shit that can possibly fuck some good shit up."

Renee rolled her eyes. "I'm just sayin', I don't need you doin' me or my kids any favors. We've been good thus long, so don't think we need any handouts."

"That right there is gon' push a nigga like me away, real talk. Just chill the fuck out and let shit run its course. Because right about now, you gettin' on my nervous ma, fareal. I say a lot of shit that I mean but, when my actions speak louder, you go wit' them shits, a'ight?" he asked.

Renee didn't say another word; she just nodded her head up and down.

"Good, now hurry up and shower. That steam got that pussy hot and bothered," Brave laughed.

"Shut up stupid!" Renee laughed as she playfully punched him and kicked him out of the bathroom.

She closed the door and then got in the shower, which was now lukewarm, but she didn't care. The only thing she could think about was the way Brave made her feel. No matter how much she attempted to push him away with her lack of confidence, there he was fighting her with positivity and showing her what coming across a real boss ass nigga was all about.

Chapter Twelve

Harmony Winfield-Miller & Renee:

Wednesday morning arrived and Renee was stocking clothes. The new arrivals had arrived early and she wanted to get a head start on getting things together for the sale they were having that Wednesday thru Friday. It was 10 a.m., and Renee knew she had a long day ahead of her. Though she didn't mind because the new girls Alexis, Tracy, and Le'Asia were on their A game.

Renee had no complaints because she could tell they were about their paper. Two of them were in their early twenties and they were in college, so they could use the extra money they were getting from the boutique, and the other was around Jasmin's age. She gave off a motherly vibe as well, but she was more so about keeping the store in order rather than worried about anything else.

She took the store serious because that's how she got her money and there were bills that needed to be paid, so no games needed to be played when it came to business, and Harmony knew she finally had the right team.

"Good morning ladies," Harmony greeted when she walked in. She was in a much better mood that day, despite what was going on in her personal life.

"Good morning Mrs. Winfield, how are you?" the ladies asked in unison.

"Blessed to see another day. How about yawl?" she asked.

"I'm good. A little tired," Alexis stated.

"Same here, school is kicking my ass. Excuse my language Mrs. Winfield, but it's the truth," Le'Asia added.

"Well, I done had my coffee for the morning, so everything is good on my end," Tracy chimed in.

Harmony chuckled. "Well, Alexis, I won't hold you all long today. We're closing at 3 p.m., considering we will be open an hour early for the sales we're having." She turned her attention to Le'Asia. "As for you, missy. School is tough, but understand that all you're doing will be worth it in the end."

"I know and thank you, Harmony. I mean Mrs. Winfield," Le'Asia corrected herself.

"Harmony is fine, honey." Harmony walked over to where Renee was stocking clothes and shoes.

"Come into my office once you're finished Renee."

Renee nodded okay before turning her attention back to what she was already doing. When Harmony got to the back, she closed the door and broke down. She was thankful enough to keep it together in front of her employees, but she was broken up inside.

Finding out that Kaotic was Chaos' brother and, on top of that, she had an affair with him, was the ultimate betrayal and she just knew there was no way she was going to get him back.

Knock.

Knock.

"Can I come in?" Renee asked from the other side of the door.

"Yea," Harmony sniffled, trying to get herself together.

Renee walked in and closed the door behind her.

"Wassup chick?"

"So, Brave called me yesterday and said you was taking the day off. Hmm, what's going on?" Harmony asked in curiosity.

She needed to hear about someone else's happiness because she was going through hell and then some.

"Girl, I had nothing to do with that. I swear. He surprised me because I was damn sure late for work when I jumped out of bed," Renee laughed.

"So, he was at your house when you woke up?"

"He stayed the night," Renee said in a nonchalant manner.

"What!" Harmony was shocked.

"Yea, that surprised me too. But, all I can say is that he is special and I look forward to seeing where things go between us. The first time I ever met a thug ass nigga with a hint of gentleman in him," Renee explained.

Harmony didn't speak, but she was happy for Renee. She could see her want for love and she was glad that she was finally getting it, and she was getting it with a good man because Brave was thorough. The more she thought about how she played matchmaker but her marriage was in shambles, it made her become very emotional, especially with the information she had been withholding from Chaos since she found out.

"Are you okay? Harmony, please don't break down again. You gotta be strong through this girl."

"Nah, Renee, this shit is much deeper than you think," Harmony spoke through her cries.

Renee sat down on the love seat in the corner and wondered what exactly was going on. She was praying that Harmony wasn't holding more secrets back because she was doing all she could to have her back and, if anything else came about, Renee was going to really have to tell Harmony about herself, no matter how blunt the truth came off.

"What can possibly be going on now Harm?"

"Chaos is going to kill me. He is going to kill me for sure once he finds out that the nigga I fucked is the same nigga that tried to take his life," Harmony confessed.

Renee's mouth fell wide open. She put her hands over her mouth in a shocked manner. She couldn't even muster up a sentence because she was truly in disbelief at what she had just found out.

"And, on top of that, Kaotic is his brother," Harmony continued to drop the bombs on Renee.

"What!" Renee exclaimed.

"I—I didn't know Renee, I swear I didn't know," Harmony cried.

Renee rubbed her forehead as she listened to Harmony's cries. There was nothing she could say or do because shit was going to hit the fan once Chaos found out. Renee couldn't even console Harmony because she was just as scared for her friend, as if it were her in the situation.

"Harmony, you have to tell him."

Harmony popped her head up from her desk. "How? How am I going to tell my husband that the man I cheated on him with is the same nigga who shot him and, oh, by the way, he's your brother? Then, on top of that, I'm not sure who I'm pregnant by?"

"It doesn't matter how you tell him. Just fuckin' tell him. This shit can't be kept on the down low because this shit is serious. Chaos could have died. And speaking of your child, what are you going to do? You haven't been to the doctors or mentioned the baby since you've been pregnant."

"I know this already, Renee. You don't have to tell me, but Chaos won't even talk to me. What am I supposed to do, beg him to talk to me? And I don't give a fuck about this baby, to be honest. I'm doing everything in my power to lose it." she said.

"Harmony, I don't give a fuck what you do or how long it takes. You need to tell Chaos what the fuck is going on. Did you know that he was the same nigga that shot him? Like, did you know you was fuckin' his brother? And what the fuck do you mean lose it? Just go get a fuckin' abortion!" Renee became frustrated.

She loved Harmony and looked up to her, but the shit that was going on was grimy and beyond deceitful. She never would have thought that this would be Harmony's character, but she wasn't liking it at all and now was the time to let her friend know how foul and fucked up she was looking.

"Hell no! I didn't know anything. I fucked up by cheating, but I wouldn't dare do any grimy shit like that. I love Chaos! But, I felt like I was losing him to the club and I got tired of it. Yea, my actions were fucked up, but it happened and I can't change it. Besides, he's fucking Brittany anyway, so why am I the only one wrong in this? And I've thought about it."

Renee rolled her eyes to the ceiling. "Girl, he ain't fuckin' that hoe."

"Oh, yes, he is. Chaos wouldn't lie on his dick. Believe me," Harmony vouched for him.

Renee waved her off. "Chaos ain't fuckin' that hoe. I don't know him like that, but that nigga heart and dick belongs to you. Believe me. He only said that to hurt you because he's hurting and he wanted you to feel how he was feeling. Don't take something he said and run with it because that's just gonna make shit worse than what it needs to be, and ya ass is already in scalding hot ass water."

Harmony just wasn't convinced. Everything Renee said sounded good, but she truly felt like Chaos had been dealing with Brittany. There was no way an old fling from back in the day would just pop up without reason, or was it?

Chaos Miller & Brittany:

"Damn, so yawl gettin' pretty close, huh?" Chaos asked.

It was around 5:25 p.m. and the club was busy, but not as busy as it would be on weekends. Normally on Mondays, Tuesdays, and Wednesdays, the club was mellow; it wasn't as packed. It was filled with a few old heads that enjoyed spending hundreds of dollars on the ladies, and Chaos nor Brave minded one bit.

"Yea, we gettin' close, but I'm not goin' to make her mines verbally until the time is right," Brave responded.

"Nigga, you done already nutted in her. The fuck you mean you ain't gon' make her yours yet," Chaos laughed while he took another pull of the blunt he was smoking and passed it to Brave.

"Shut the fuck up," Brave laughed as he took the blunt. "I'm sayin', I already know she mines, but she don't know that. I just feel like since you and sis ain't on good terms, it'll be fucked up for me to be all mushy and shit wit' Renee."

Chaos got quiet as he leaned back in his swivel chair. The situation between him and Harmony was still unbelievable to him but, whenever it was mentioned or whenever he thought about it, he realized it was his reality.

"I ain't mean to blow ya high bruh," Brave said, noticing Chaos' mood change.

"Nah, you good bruh. Shit between me and Harmony ain't got nothin' to do wit' you, so don't stop ya life. I understand what you sayin' and I appreciate ya loyalty to me, but don't stop what could be a good thing, just because me and Harmony are no longer together. Besides, Renee gotta be special because you fuckin' a bitch raw? Nah, that's never you, so it's def' somethin' there that you afraid to admit."

Brave chuckled. "I just don't feel right. I looked up to you and sis relationship, so all this shit that happened just been blowin' me and, then on top of that, Renee could do the same shit to me. I mean, you just never know and that's some shit I ain't got time for because you know how I am. I'm really fuckin' trigger happy. I been done blew her damn head off or punched it off. Either or, it damn sure don't make me no never mind," Brave stated seriously.

"You crazy as fuck bruh, but don't let what-"

Knock.

Knock.

Chaos and Braves conversation was cut short when Coroner walked in.

"Sorry to interrupt yawl but, boss man, a young lady by the name of Brittany is here to speak with you," he said.

Both Brave and Chaos looked at each other. Chaos shook his head because Brittany was just doing too much for his taste, and he told her before that he wasn't with the stalker shit that she was on.

"Are you serious?" Chaos asked, just to make sure.

"I wouldn't lie boss man," Coroner assured.

"This bitch gon' make me push her shit back." Chaos blew loudly as he got up out of his swivel chair, walked around the desk, and pushed past Coroner.

He walked down the mini hallway and into the club, where he saw Brittany standing over by the bar. Candy poked out her lips and raised her eye brows at Chaos as he walked up. He knew for a face that the next time Harmony came in, she would find out that Brittany was at the club, and that was something that he did not need. Granted, he and Harmony was done but, regardless of how Harmony did him, it was just certain lines of disrespect he did not cross.

"What the fuck you doin' here yo?" Chaos got straight to the point when he walked up.

"Is that any way to greet me?" Brittany asked.

"Fuck all that." Chaos waved her off. "What the fuck are you doin' here?" he asked again.

"I wanted to talk and I knew you would be working, so I decided to stop by," she told him.

By this time, Brave and Coroner had just entered the club area. Brittany smiled at Brave and waved at him, in which he responded with a simple nod. He didn't want to be involved with Brittany and her bullshit because last time, Harmony snapped on him and, although she wasn't there at that very moment, that was just something he ain't have time for.

"Talk about what? The fuck is so important that got you poppin' up at my job?" Chaos barked.

Brittany placed her hand on her hip and rolled her neck as she spoke. "Don't fuckin' act like we can't have a conversation. I told you that I was going through some things, and you gave me the okay concerning us hanging out. So, now I'm here and don't you dare try to deny me, just because we're in your place of business."

Candy was taking everything in, and Chaos noticed it. He looked back at Brave and waved him over.

"Wassup?" Brave asked when he walked over.

"I'm about to get her the fuck away from here. Hold it down until I get back, a'ight?" Chaos asked.

"Oh, most def'. You know I got you, bro," Brave assured him as he gave Chaos dap.

"Thanks, bruh," Chaos said before turning back to Brittany. "Let's go yo."

Brittany turned her head and smiled at Brittany before winking at Brave. All Brave could do was shake his head, but he didn't say anything. Candy, on the other hand, flipped her the bird and continued serving drinks. She was just the bartender, but she knew a snake ass bitch when she came across one, and she could tell that Harmony and Chaos had been going through something because she hadn't been seeing Harmony at the club. She was going to stay in her place but, if she ever saw Harmony at the club again, she was most certainly going to let her know about Brittany's pop up.

***

Harmony Winfield- Miller & Casey Miller:

Harmony didn't close the boutique down until 7:00 p.m. The sale started the moment the new inventory was restocked, and she was thankful that she gave Renee access to the website because she did an email blast and the store was flooded like roaches when the lights came on. Harmony was tired, but she had one stop to make before she went. It took her a good thirty minutes before she arrived at Casey's house in Buena, New Jersey. It was just on the outskirts of Vineland where she and Chaos lived, so it wasn't too much out of her way. But, she didn't care if it was because there were just a few things that Harmony needed to get to the bottom of, before she went to Chaos and revealed what she knew.

Harmony pulled into the driveway of Casey's single-family home and turned off her car. She didn't bother taking her purse with her when she got out because she didn't plan on being there long, and Casey lived in a pretty decent neighborhood. Besides, even if someone did try anything, the alarm on her car would go off the moment somebody tried grabbing the handle. She got out of the car and walked up the mini ramp that led to her doorway.

Knock. Knock.

Knock.

"One second chile! I don't know why you don't use your damn key. I'm tired of getting up and opening the damn door for you!" Casey snapped.

Harmony could hear her coming to the door. She chuckled a little at Casey's fussing, but she turned her game face on quickly when Casey opened the door.

"Oh, Harmony. I didn't expect you. I thought you were Chaos. Is something wrong?" she asked.

"Sure is, we need to talk," Harmony stated firmly.

"Alright, well come in." Casey moved to the side to let Harmony come inside.

Harmony walked past her, and Casey followed and then closed the door behind them.

"Do you want anything to drink? Coffee? Tea? Juice? Water?"

"No, I don't want anything to drink, but I do want to know why you never told Chaos he had a brother. A twin brother at that," Harmony blurted out.

Casey raised her eye brows as she looked at Harmony. She didn't know how Harmony knew about the secret she kept since the birth of her twins, but she wasn't too happy about it.

"Chile, now, don't you come in here questioning me about my business that doesn't concern you," Casey was defensive.

"When it concerns my husband, it does concern me," Harmony shot back.

"Husband?" Casey said in a high-pitched tone.

"Yes, husband! I know I screwed up by cheating on Chaos, but he is still my husband and, right now, I want answers. Kaotic came to me and told me how him and Chaos is brothers. I bet you're wondering how in the entire hell do I know Kaotic? Well, he's the guy I've been sleeping with behind Chaos back. Do you know how trashy that makes me look? Not only did I cheat, but to find out I cheated with my husband's twin brother is a fucking disgrace!" Harmony explained with anger in each word.

She didn't mean to use profanity towards Casey, but shit was getting out of hand due to all the lies that were being told, including hers.

"Harmony, there's a lot that you don't understand," Casey stated.

Casey didn't focus on the fact that Kaotic was the man Harmony was sleeping with. She was more so focused on her secret getting out before she wanted it to, and the fact that Harmony knew about it made her very uneasy.

"Well, please make me understand? Because Chaos is going to kill me when he finds out about this. It's bad enough I cheated and he wants a divorce, but cheating with his brother? A brother he never knew about and you knew about it all? This shit looks bad and its gonna get worse." Harmony shook her head.

"I understand everything you're saying, and I know what you did was a mistake. Kaotic is angry at me for giving him up for adoption and not both of them. I couldn't afford to take care of two children, I just couldn't. Their father was in the streets bad, and I couldn't risk having the streets taking my children. It's hard for black men out here, and I refused to see both of my children go down the same path as their father so, yes, I gave Kaotic up for adoption and took the chance with Chaos. It was wrong, but I did what I had to do," Casey explained.

"I can't blame you for the decision you made, but why not tell Chaos? This man tried to kill Chaos because of something you did. I know I messed up, but he is seeking those that Chaos loves, just to break him. When is it going to end, Casey?" Harmony asked as tears filled her eyes.

"I'm so sorry Harmony. I should've told Chaos a long time ago, but he was already going through so much with the death of his father and me barely being able to make ends meet. Those streets got ahold of him and I just never got the courage to tell him the truth," she said.

Harmony combed her fingers through her hair and sighed loudly, as she walked past Casey and took a seat.

"How did he make contact with you again? Like, when did it happen, hell, how did it happen?" she wanted to know.

Casey took a seat at the dining room table and didn't waste any time telling Harmony how she and Kaotic reconnected.

Casey was in the kitchen preparing herself a small breakfast.

She heard a car pull in her driveway, just as she was flipping the last of the pancakes she made. Immediately, she thought it was Chaos, so she decided to meet him at the door, considering he never used his key. Casey wiped her hands off on her apron and opened the door. She saw an all-black 2015 Bentley and assumed that Chaos had purchased a new car but, when the man emerged from the car, she knew that she had quickly mistaken.

She placed her hand on her chest, as if she was having trouble breathing. Despite the fact that she didn't raise him and it had been many years since she saw him, a mother knew her child.

"My God." She was shocked and nervous. "What are you doing here?"

Casey knew who Kaotic was, but she clearly didn't know him as a person because at that moment, he felt disrespected.

"That's all you gon' say?" he asked. He was mean mugging her and, not to mention, his guard was already up, but now he was in defense mode.

"I-I'm sorry. It's just been so long, and I didn't expect this. Come on in chile," her reaction was a bit softer this time.

Kaotic closed his car door and walked up the mini ramp. Casey held the door open and allowed him to walk into her home.

"Are you hungry? You came just in time for some breakfast," Casey said as she shut the door behind him.

Kaotic looked around the kitchen briefly and approved it in his head. It was warm and cozy, and it even made him think about the many dinners he missed growing up.

"Nah, I'm straight," he responded, although his stomach was growling; eating was not what he came there for.

"Well, you look real nice. You've grown to be a handsome young man," she complimented.

He didn't thank her; instead, they both just looked back at one another for a few minutes.

Neither one of them knew exactly what to say at that moment.

"Why don't you come into the living room, so we can talk a little," Casey suggested with a warm smile.

Kaotic agreed and followed her into the living room, and they both took a seat on her couch. There was an awkward silence that filled the room, so Casey decided to try and break the ice.

"How's life been treating you?"

Kaotic's mouth wanted to respond, but his eyes were too busy wandering around her well-furnished living room. There were so many pictures of Chaos and Casey together. Even a few pictures of who he assumed to be their father, but not one picture of him was present.

"So, that's ya family, huh?" he asked, nodding towards a few of the pictures.

Casey swallowed hard. "Let's not talk about those pictures. I want to see how you're doing."

"Why? You ain't give a fuck then. So, don't give a fuck now," Kaotic's demeanor changed and he was acting like himself now.

"Listen here chile. I know you may be upset, but I'm not going to have you talking to me any kind of way. You gon' show me some respect in my house. Do you understand?"

"Pssh!" Kaotic waved her off. "I ain't tryna hear none of that bullshit you talkin'. Now, I asked you a question. Is that ya muthafuckin' family?"

"Yes! Yes, that's my family. It's your family too. I understand that you have a lot of anger but, baby, taking it out on me ain't going to solve a damn thing. I made a huge mistake back then and I prayed to God about it every day. Please forgive me," she begged.

Seeing the picture of Chaos bothered Kaotic something serious. He couldn't understand how his mother could give away her own flesh and blood, let alone split up a set of twins.

"Fuck all that forgiveness shit. You gave me away and kept that nigga?" he snapped.

"It wasn't like that. I just wasn't prepared to take care of two children. I swear to you, it wasn't easy. I struggled every day of my life, and I knew giving you up would allow you to have a better life."

Kaotic rubbed his hands down his face and then stood up. A part of him wanted to spit on Casey and maybe even punch her, but he knew physical pain wasn't going to solve anything. He wanted her to feel the way he felt for so many years: empty and alone, with no one to turn to. Kaotic knew that his father was no longer living, so his only other target was Chaos.

Fuck that nigga, he thought.

"A better life huh? You sound dumb as fuck. I'ma get the fuck up outta here before I cause bodily harm to you and, believe me, I'ma certified maniac in these muthafuckin' streets, so it ain't nothin' for me to off a bitch who mean shit to me."

Kaotic turned to walk away.

"Kaotic!" Casey called out to him.

He stopped in his tracks, but he never looked back.

"I'm sorry son. I truly am, but you have to put yourself in my shoes. I just couldn't take care of the both of you. Times was hard back then. You have to understand that I always loved you and that I did what I felt was best," she tried her hardest to explain.

He chuckled as he shook his head. "You should've gave us both up. Not just one."

Kaotic said what he had to say and walked out, leaving Casey to stand there in her sorrow. She wanted to chase after Kaotic, but she knew it was best to let him go. Casey prayed that they could have another conversation someday and, that, this time, Chaos could be present, so they could get to know one another. But, little did she know, Kaotic was about to introduce himself to Chaos real soon.

When Casey finished telling Harmony about the reuniting of her and her long-lost son, Harmony just shook her head. Just by the words Kaotic spoke to Casey, she knew that he was going to do everything in his power to cause Chaos pain.

"So, what did you do after yawl talked?" Harmony asked.

"I prayed. That's all I could do," Casey responded.

Harmony frowned her face up and cocked her head to the side in a *bitch are you serious* manner.

"Prayed? Casey, you can't be serious right now? You didn't think to tell Chaos about any of this? This man is crazy, and I'm not saying this to get my ass outta hot water. Kaotic is crazy!"

"Harmony, don't you think I know that! He came to me and told me he shot Chaos, but I didn't have the courage to tell my son the truth. I know I'm wrong and I play a big part in this, but my son has been through hell and back. I can't see him go back to the old Chaos. I prayed long and hard for many years for him to turn his life around, and he finally did. So, if me keeping secrets will keep him on the right path, then so be it," Casey cried.

"What do you mean he came to you and told you he shot Chaos? Casey, you mean you knew before me and you didn't say anything?" Harmony asked as tears formed in her eyes.

Both she and Casey had betrayed Chaos so deep that she didn't know if he could or would ever be able to forgive them. She hated that she was a part of such a fucked-up situation, but she made her bed and now she had to lie in it.

"When you went to New York, I found out the night before you came back. Chaos was asleep when Kaotic came to the house."

Harmony raised an eye brow. "He came to our home?" she asked.

Casey nodded. "Yes, I don't know how he knew where yawl lived, but he came there and didn't have a care in the world about doing so," Casey stated.

"Casey, do you know that if Chaos finds out that this man came to our home, then it's gonna be a war you will have no control over. On top of that, he's the same nigga that shot him. Chaos is going to kill him, Casey, and you won't be able to do anything about it. He ain't gonna give two shits about them being blood brothers." Harmony wiped the tears that had fell from her eyes.

"I didn't want it to come to this but, after the second conversation me and Kaotic had, I just felt like whatever happens, happens," she said.

"What did he say?" Harmony wanted to know everything because she was going to be the one to go to Chaos because Casey wasn't bold enough, and her keeping things in was causing the situation to be worse.

"I was cooking dinner when..."

A light beamed from outside of the house and Casey put her hand up as she squinted her eyes. She got up off the sofa and went to the door and opened it. Someone was sitting outside of the driveway with their high beams on. She turned the outside light on to see if she could get a closer look, but that just made it worse.

After a few seconds, the lights when off and she almost shit her pants when she saw Kaotic sitting behind the wheel of the car. She wanted to slam the door, lock it, and run upstairs, but only God knows what he may have done if she would have run from him. She repeatedly looked behind her as she closed the door.

When she got to the driver's side of the car, she peeked at him.

"What do you want from me? What are you doing here? How did you even know where my son lived?" Casey asked him twenty-one questions.

"I'm giving you a chance to make things right," Kaotic said.

"What do you mean?" Casey asked in confusion. She didn't even care that he didn't answer her other questions.

"Go inside and tell Chaos the truth right now, and I will leave you alone for good," he told her.

Casey hesitated, but then thought on it for a moment. Both she and Chaos had come way too far, and they had survived a lot of trials and tribulations; however, she couldn't find it in herself to tell him the truth about Kaotic. From what he knew, he was an only child and that was exactly how she liked to keep it.

"Kaotic, why can't you just allow me to go to him when I'm ready, instead of trying to force me to do something? I don't want any drama, okay? It's bad enough that my son got shot and that didn't happen until you paid me a visit," Casey said.

"Hint, hint," Kaotic shot back.

Casey's chest felt like it was tightening up on her, so she placed her hand up against it.

"Lord, I knew it. I knew you did this. Why Kaotic, why? He's your brother!" Casey's tone got loud and she quickly looked towards the house. "He's your brother, Kaotic. You could have killed him!"

Casey's voice was a bit quieter this time around.

"Brother, huh? Well, he don't know that and, until he does, I'ma bring pain to this whole muthafuckin' family," Kaotic threatened.

"I will tell him. Just give me time. Please just give me time but, whatever you do, don't hurt him again," Casey begged.

Kaotic smirked.

"I can tell you care about him way more than you care about me. The fact of the matter is that you're trying to save face. You wanna continue to look like a fuckin' saint and you kept me in the dark while trying to do so. I tell you one thing; if you don't tell him, I will, and you can bet your bottom dollar that when I approach him, it's gon' be more than guns blazing." Kaotic put his car in reverse and pulled out of the driveway wildly, leaving Casey to stand there alone.

"And you gonna say whatever happens, happens? Casey, I cannot deal with you right now. It's like you don't even care about Chaos," Harmony said once Casey was finished telling her what happened.

"It's not that I don't care. I can't control those two when it comes to things like this. The best thing I can do is talk to them and try to have them talk things out, rather than shoot it out."

"But, you started it. If only you would have told the truth from jump, none of this would have happened. So, not only am I a cheater, I also slept with my husband's twin brother. Not only are you a liar, but you're the cause of this." Harmony didn't give a fuck how Casey felt. She gave it to her straight with no chaser.

Just then, Casey and Harmony was both interrupted when the door opened. When Chaos and Harmony's eyes met, anger appeared in his face.

"What the fuck is she doin' here yo?" he snapped.

"What the fuck is that bitch doing here with you!" Harmony shot back when she saw Brittany walking in behind Chaos.

"Chaos, she just came to talk," Casey intervened. She could see the calm before the storm and she wanted to squash things before it got out of hand.

"You're my mother-in-law. I can come by here whenever I damn well please. Now, why the fuck is that bitch walking in with you?" Harmony said.

"You got one more time to call me a bitch!" Brittany warned as she stood beside Chaos.

"And, bitch, what the fuck you gonna do?" Harmony asked as she took a few steps closer and crossed her arms across her chest.

She was just waiting for Brittany to feel froggy and leap because she was going to tear Casey's house up by whooping ass.

"If me and you on bad terms Harmony, I don't want you here," Chaos said but, this time, his voice was a little more at ease. He was focused on keeping the two women that stood before him apart.

"She needs to understand that when you fuck up with your man, you make way for the next woman to come in and make shit right," Brittany snickered.

Smack!

Chaos, Casey, nor Brittany saw it coming but, it one swift motion, Harmony punched Brittany dead in her mouth. The punch was so vicious, it gave Brittany whiplash. Chaos didn't catch heads or tails of what was going on until Brittany's head snapped back, and Harmony was on her like white on rice.

"Bitch, I'll tear you apart in here!" Harmony snapped while she took a handful of Brittany's hair and snatched her towards her direction.

"Harmony, let her go!" Chaos yelled.

Smack!

Smack!

Chaos had a grip on Harmony's hand as he tried to break the ladies up. With her free hand, she managed to pop Brittany two more good times.

"I'll kill this bitch!" Harmony screamed.

Chaos didn't feel like struggling with Harmony, so he bear-hugged her and scooped her up in the air, hoping that would get her off Brittany.

Grrrr!

"Ahhhhhhh! She's biting me! This bitch is biting me!" Brittany screamed.

Those were the first words she could get out since the physical altercation started. She was more focused on trying to get Harmony off her, and she was still dizzy from the first hit she took from Harmony.

"Harmony, stop! What the fuck man!" Chaos yelled as he pulled Harmony but, the more he pulled Harmony, the more she bit down on Brittany's arm.

Harmony was latched on to Brittany like a Pitbull. Everything in her wanted to kill Brittany and, since she couldn't do that, she was going to take her damn arm off or at least try to.

"Harmony, baby, let her go," Casey said in a soft tone. She stood back when everything kicked off, but she knew sooner or later the ladies were going to get at one another.

"Harmony, let her go yo fareal! This shit is crazy!" Chaos said as he tried to stop Harmony from biting Brittany.

His back was to Brittany, but Harmony had her armed pulled around Chaos as she bit her. Casey walked over and gently placed her hand on Harmony's forehead as she gently pulled Brittany's arm.

"Harmony, sweetie. Let her go, this is Casey talking to you. Please let her go," Casey begged.

Brittany was getting light headed and she dropped to the floor, and that was when Harmony let go.

Thump!

"Bum ass bitch! I'ma whoop ya ass every time I see you, hoe! You ain't never gonna have Chaos!"

Harmony managed to kick Brittany before Chaos could walk her into the living room.

"What the fuck is wrong with you?" he asked.

Casey ran to the bathroom quickly and grabbed some peroxide, the first aid kit, and a white washcloth.

"That bitch shouldn't be around you and you shouldn't be with her! You gon' disrespect me like that?"

"Disrespect? You wanna talk about disrespect? Do you really wanna go there, Harmony?" he asked.

"I don't give a fuck! I put in too much work to allow a bitch that will never compare to me to come and take my spot! Then, for you to tell me you fuckin' this bitch? That's how we doing our time. This bitch ain't got shit on me and this the same bitch I had to deal with before, when you was in the streets! What the fuck did you do? You left her dumb ass alone when you found out I was the real and she was a snake ass bitch!"

Chaos wiped his hands down his face. He was more than frustrated because of the situation. He felt like both Brittany and Harmony was wrong for what went down tonight.

"Well, I guess yawl got somethin' in common," Chaos said before leaving Harmony standing in the living room alone.

"Is she good? I'm take her to the hospital, and just tell Brave to come pick me up because I'ma take her in her car," Chaos said to his mother.

"She definitely needs to be seen. A nice chunk is gone from her arm, and I think Harmony needs to go too, just so she can get checked," Casey suggested.

Chaos shook his head. "I be damned if I keep breakin' up fights all night. She gon' have to go on her own time. She ain't fucked up like this," Chaos said.

"I apologize for this Casey," Brittany whimpered, as Chaos helped her out of the chair she was now sitting in.

"Baby, just go on and get yourself fixed up," Casey told her.

"You really gon' leave with that bitch!" Harmony called out.

"Shut the fuck up! I'm takin' her to the hospital!" Chaos barked.

"I don't give a fuck! Let that bitch bleed to death!" Harmony spat.

Chaos knew that, if he responded, he and Harmony was going to get into a full-blown argument. So, he knew his best bet was to just get Brittany and leave.

"Chaos, I swear if you walk out of that door with that bitch, I'ma make sure the next time I whoop her ass, I do more damage!" Harmony threatened.

Chaos sighed deeply and left out of the house with Brittany by his side. He knew Harmony was good on her threats but, he felt since he brought Brittany into the ass whooping she'd just received, the least he could do was take her to the hospital.

***

Chaos Miller & Brittany:

"Ma bad about all this," Chaos said to Brittany as they waited to be seen by the doctor. They were in room number four in the emergency room at the Inspira Medical Center in Vineland, New Jersey.

"You could have done more to stop it. Look at my arm Chaos? And the nerve of her to say the shit she said. I swear, I can't wait until I see that bitch again," Brittany said with flared nostrils. She was getting upset all over again and, on top of that, her arm was in excruciating pain.

"The fuck you mean I should have done more to stop it? Why the fuck did you say what you said? That's why she snapped on you the way that she did. Don't flip the shit and put it on me like I was the one who bit a chunk out of ya arm."

"If we're dealing, you should do what you have to, to protect me. I felt like I had every right to say what I said, and you should have backed me. I'm not dumb; I know you and Harmony ain't together because you've been spending too much time at your mother's house," Brittany said.

Chaos looked at Brittany with a crazed look because she was clearly bugged out. "Since when were we dealing? And why the hell wasn't I notified about this? You crazy as fuck if you think I'ma choose you over ma damn wife. Get the fuck outta here wit' that bullshit. I'm not about to involve myself in some shit that you started."

"Whatever Chaos. You really need to know whose down for you and who's not. I refuse to be put on the back burner again," Brittany said.

Chaos wanted to respond but in walked the doctor, so he bit his tongue.

"Hello, how are you? I'm Dr. Puccini, and what seems to be the problem today?"

"I'm fine and yourself? And I got into an altercation and I was bit bad," she explained.

"Yikes, that is a pretty bad bite. We're going to give you a shot for any infection or pain, and then we're going to stitch you up," Dr. Puccini explained.

"Okay, thank you," Brittany said.

"It's no problem. My job is to make sure you leave out of here better than how you came in," Dr. Puccini said before walking out.

As soon as the doctor walked out, Chaos was back on the conversation they were having.

"Brittany, I'ma tell you like I told you before. I'm never fuckin' wit' you on that level again. You keep tryna pretend we in this relationship, when we not. Stop it, fareal, before shit get outta hand," he said in a firm tone.

Brittany rolled her eyes. She ignored every last word that Chaos was saying because she knew that if he didn't want her around, then she wouldn't be around but, in her mind, she was there and that's exactly where he wanted her to be.

Chapter Thirteen

Jasmin and Kaotic Miller:

It had been three long months, and Jasmin was more than miserable. She had given her son away, lost her job at Love and Harmony boutique, stopped dealing with Crystal, and was on bad terms with the love of her life. Things were truly bad for her and, the more stress she endured, the older she looked.

"Kaotic, I can't do this anymore," she said as she watched him get dressed.

He glanced back at her while putting on his shirt. "What you talkin' about?" he asked.

"It's Saturday, July first, and you know how many times you came by to see me?" she asked.

"Don't start this shit Jasmin," Kaotic quickly replied.

"What do you mean don't start this shit? I'm tired of being in a part-time relationship. I love you more than life itself and I don't understand why you just can't see that. What is it that I have to do in order to prove my love to you?" Jasmin spoke from the heart, and she was hoping Kaotic heard her.

Kaotic looked up at the ceiling and sighed long and hard. "You'll do anything to prove ya love to me?" he asked.

"Yes baby, anything," Jasmin told him.

"Cool, that's def' wassup. Daddy need you to do a few things for me, a'ight," Kaotic said.

"Anything baby," Jasmin told him.

"Tell me what happened the day after you found out I was fuckin' Harmony," Kaotic said.

"Why?" Jasmin asked.

"Because I received a text message sayin' yawl got into it, so tell me wassup?"

"Kaotic, that was so long ago," Jasmin laughed as if he was playing, when he clearly wasn't.

"I don't give a fuck how long ago it was. I stopped talkin' to ya ass, which is why I'm just now confrontin' you about the shit; now, tell me what the fuck happened," Kaotic said.

"We didn't fight the same day! It was the day after!" Jasmin yelled.

"I don't give a fuck when yawl fought. Tell me the whole fuckin' story! Why the fuck you keep playin' wit' me? I'ma punch a fuckin' hole in ya face if you keep on talkin' back after I told you to do somethin'," Kaotic warned.

Jasmin cleared her throat before she explained the situation word for word. She started out with her and Crystal's little dinner date.

"Girl, you sounded so upset on the phone. What's going on?" Crystal's facial expression was concerned but, inside, she was eager to get the tea.

Jasmin took another sip of martini before sitting it down. "Order you a drink first because you are damn sure going to need it."

"Oh shit, this must be juicier than I thought," she said as she sat down.

"It definitely is," Jasmin added.

Crystal waved for the waitress to come over, so she could get herself a drink or two.

"Hi, my name is Natalie. How are you?" the waitress asked.

Crystal frowned at how happy and extra the waitress was acting.

"*Girl, calm down a bit but, anyway, just give me a Strawberry Dakari and a shot of V.S.O.P.*"

The waitress was still looking goofy, but one could see the embarrassment of her getting checked written all over her face.

"*Okay. I'll be right back.*" Natalie walked away.

"*Alright, so while we wait for my drinks. What in the hell is going on, and what the hell happened to your eye?*" she asked.

Jasmin touched her face. "*You can still see it? I tried to cover it up with make-up. Ugh, I'm so fucking pissed right now.*"

Just as Crystal was about to say something, the waitress came back with her drinks.

"*Here you go ma'am. Anything else?*"

Crystal waved her off. "*No, we're good.*"

The waitress gave a slight smile before walking away.

"*Now, back to you. Hell yea, I can see it, so what happened?*" she repeated.

"*I'm quitting my job because that slut Harmony is a snake.*" Jasmin shook her head as she took another sip of her drink.

"Shit, I already knew that. That is nothing new," Crystal stated.

Jasmin shook her head no. "Uh uh, this trick is sleeping with my man," she revealed.

Crystal's mouth was wide open in shock. "Bitch, shut the front door. You lying!"

"I wish I was lying. Tell me why I invited my man over, and I ran him a shower while I was finishing up dinner. So, while he's in the shower, I hear his phone ring and, considering I'm his woman, I went to go answer it. Only it was a text message from Harmony saying she needed to see him because she didn't like the way she ended things went after they had spent the night together," Jasmin gave Crystal the run down.

All Crystal could do was pause on her Strawberry Dakari and take her shot of V.S.O.P. She couldn't stand Harmony, but never in her life would she had thought that she was sleeping with her employee's man.

"Okay, a few things. Why in the hell are you inviting your man over to dinner? And what the hell do you mean they spent the night together? Oh, hell naw, to the naw, naw, naw!"

"That's not the fucking point Crystal! This bitch is sleeping with my man. I can't let her get away with this. I just can't," Jasmin cried.

Crystal was in awe. She was enjoying the tea she was getting, but she didn't want to see Jasmin hurting.

"Let me guess. You confronted him, and the result was you getting your eye blacked? That's a damn shame girl. You did not deserve that at all and, if he wants Harmony so bad, then let him have her cheating ass. You can do so much better," Crystal told her.

Jasmin frowned up her face. "Oh, hell no! I worked too hard to keep Kaotic. I refuse to let this bitch just take him away from me. I've been with him going on seven months and I'm not about to let some homewrecking little bitch mess us up."

Crystal was confused and her facial expression proved it. "Girl, you're older than me and the fact that you even said some shit like that got my mind all the way blown. But, hey, if you like it, then I love it; furthermore, I say you fuck up the bitch's boutique. That damn store is her pride and damn joy. I said we both knock her ass off her pedestal."

"I don't know about that Crystal." Jasmin was hesitant.

"Why not? I mean, it's the perfect plan. You already know I'm the one that opens the store, so we can do that shit and be out without a problem. She deserves it and you know it. Stop being a coward and start fighting back. Harmony thinks her shit doesn't stink and I think it's time we let her know that she ain't better than us," Crystal stated.

"So, she encouraged you to fuck Harmony's shop up, and you listened?" he asked as he laughed.

"What's funny? And you sayin' that like I couldn't have thought of something like that myself," she responded with much attitude.

"You not smart like that but, anyway, continue. Tell me what happened when yawl fought," Kaotic told her.

Jasmin rolled her eyes, but she didn't give Kaotic anymore lip. She began to tell him about the fight, and that was a day she couldn't forget a situation like that because she carried that ass whooping and so did Crystal.

"Harmony!"

Renee called out to her so that she could have her guard up.

Whap!

Jasmin swung and side snuffed Harmony because she managed to move way before the hit fully connected. After Harmony's personal space was invaded and she was physically assaulted, it was now on and popping.

"Bitch, you got me fucked up!" Harmony yelled as she went into full beast mode.

Whap! Pop! Smack!

She hit Jasmin with a mean combo, causing her nose to start bleeding instantly. Jasmin stumbled back and fell to the ground.

"Oh, hell no!" Crystal yelled as she got out of the passenger side of Jasmin's car.

Renee raised her eye brow and wondered what the hell Crystal was about to do. When she saw her trying to walk over, she stopped her.

"Uh, uh, trick where you going?"

Crystal and Renee had beef since day one. They were both waiting for the opportunity to go at each other's necks, and today was the day. The only problem was that Renee was a gutter chick and *about that life so, when Crystal knucked, Renee bucked back.*

Pop! Pop!

Whack! Whap!

Renee didn't give Crystal a chance to get ahold of her or the best of her. She could feel the heat rising between them and that was all she needed. There was no hair pulling on Renee's end. She was swinging as she bobbed and weaved in the middle of the street.

"Come on yawl, break it up!" an elderly man said as he watched the ladies fight one another.

Harmony was in mid-stomp when she noticed a crowd forming. She snapped out of the rage she was in and realized what she was doing. She looked down at Jasmin, who was laid out on the ground.

"Bitch, you got me all out here looking crazy! What the fuck is your problem!" Harmony asked.

Jasmin wiped the blood from her mouth. "You fucking my man, bitch! That's the problem, you stuck-up ass hoe."

Harmony frowned up her face. "Who the hell is your man, bitch, because the only man I'm fucking is my husband, Chaos?"

"You a lying son of a bitch! Kaotic is my man and I saw the text messages. That's why I came back to whoop your ass!" Jasmin screamed at her.

Renee pushed Crystal down on the ground. "Stay down bitch!"

She heard what had just come out of Jasmin's mouth and saw that people were standing around. She didn't want Harmony's reputation to be ruined, so she rushed to the other side of the car and forced Harmony in.

"Let's go! We don't got time for no lying ass bitches to be throwing dirt on your name."

"You not built like that, so it was Crystal that put you up to it fight as well, right?" he asked.

"What do you mean I'm not built like that? She was fucking my man, so I had to do what I had to do," Jasmin shot back.

"Ya old ass don't even sound right talkin' like that, so I know that bitch Crystal put you up to it. I never liked that bitch anyhow and, sooner or later, I'ma let her know about herself." Kaotic made a mental note.

"Why don't you like Crystal? And we don't talk anymore anyhow," Jasmin stated.

"Because that bitch was always puttin' shit in ya head. I read them fuckin messages in ya phone," Kaotic said.

"Baby, she just be talking. I don't listen to her when it comes to you."

"Yea, okay. Well, if that's the case, show me how much you love a nigga." Kaotic was still standing up when he pulled his dick out.

"Come here, and I'll show you," Jasmin purred.

"Nah bitch, come get on ya muthafuckin' knees and suck this dick," Kaotic demanded.

Jasmin didn't like how he spoke to her, but she didn't dare speak on it. She did as she was told, got off the bed, and proceeded to walk over to where he was standing.

"No bitch, crawl!" he ordered.

"Kaotic, I am not crawling over to you," Jasmin told him.

"If you don't crawl over here and suck this dick, I swear I'ma walk out this muthafucka, and you'll never hear from me again," he threatened.

Jasmin couldn't risk losing Kaotic again. Although they were back dealing, they were still rocky and she didn't want to mess things up again, so she got on her knees and began to crawl over to where he was standing. Her knees burned a bit from rubbing them across the carpet as she crawled.

"Open that mouth and swallow my shit," he told her.

Jasmin opened her mouth as wide as she could and took about a good half of Kaotic's dick in her mouth, before he grabbed the back of her head and fucked her face and throat.

"Urrrggggh," Jasmin gagged.

"Yea, gag on this dick."

Jasmin tried to push Kaotic back, but he slapped her hand away with his free hand.

"Don't fuckin' touch me. As a matter of fact, put ya hands behind ya back and lock them shits together," he told her.

Jasmin didn't understand why Kaotic was being so demanding to her and treating her like a whore, but she didn't question him or protest against it. She did as she was told and put her hands behind her and locked them together.

"Urrrrrr."

Jasmin's eyes watered, as Kaotic continuously fucked her throat as pre-semen and saliva ran down her chin.

"Ummmm," he moaned. "You love this dick, don't you?"

Jasmin nodded her head, and she bobbed it back and forth.

"You gon' do anything for me?" he asked.

She nodded again.

"You'd take a bullet for me?"

Jasmin's eyes got big, but she still nodded.

"That's my girl. Pretty soon, I'ma need you to handle some business for me. Oooh, shit," he moaned as he tried to explain what he needed done.

Kaotic couldn't hold his nut back any longer. He grabbed both sides of Jasmin's head and pulled her close so that his dick was touching the back of her throat.

"Urgh! Uhhhhh!" he growled as he released every last drop of his load down her throat.

He pulled away and watched as Jasmin swallowed what he gave her. Kaotic was weak, so he stumbled back against the wall until he got his leg strength back.

"Get yaself cleaned up because we got some talkin' to do," he said.

"What do you need my help on? Tell me now?" Jasmin was eager to know, since he asked her would she take a bullet for him.

"Nothing major. I just need you to be a getaway driver. Now, like I said, go get cleaned up because we got some talkin' to do."

Jasmin wasn't into the street life, but she watched a lot of movies, and she knew that Kaotic was up to no good when he said he needed her as a getaway driver. She would never deny him help, but she truly questioned how much she was risking in order to please such a man like Kaotic.

***

Chaos Miller & Casey Miller:

Chaos was in the kitchen finishing up cooking a late brunch for him and Casey. It had been such a long time since they really had any mother and son time and he decided that today was the day.

Chaos had been living with her since April. It was now July, and he was actually handling things a lot better when it came to his recent break up. Harmony tried reaching out to him many times to talk and work through things, but he just wasn't for it. He couldn't find himself being back with he, not after all that she's done.

"Mmm, something smells good. What did I do to deserve such wonderful treatment?" Casey joked when she came out of the bedroom.

Chaos had cooked waffles, grilled steak, grits, eggs, ham, and set out fresh fruit. Casey had been relaxing all day while Chaos took over the house duties, and she enjoyed every bit of it.

"Aw, don't try to play me ma," Chaos told her.

He heard his phone go off, and he looked down at it to see a text notification. He opened his phone and saw that it was from Harmony.

Harmony: *Chaos please unblock me. We need to talk. It's important.*

Chaos: *Do you need any money? Something wrong with the house?*

"Chile, all I'm sayin' is I can't remember the last time you cooked. I bet Harmony would say the same thing," she laughed.

Chaos didn't respond. He just set the table and began fixing both him and Casey's plates. He motioned for Casey to sit down and, when she did, he pushed her chair in and then took a seat himself. Chaos poured them both a glass of orange juice and then grabbed his mother's hand.

Harmony: *No, but I need to talk to you.*

Chaos ignored her text and looked at his mother.

"Wanna lead us in prayer?" he asked.

All Casey could do was smile because it had been so long since they did anything like this. She could remember back when Chaos was younger and she would come home from work and dinner was either done or almost done. Chaos would get in the kitchen and whip up whatever was in there at the time.

"God is great! God is good! Let us thank Him For our food. Amen!"

"Amen," Chaos said.

"So, what's going on?" Casey asked as she stuck a forkful of eggs into her mouth.

"Why you ask that?" he wanted to know.

"Because I'm your mother and I know you only do this when you have a lot on your mind," Casey said as she cut a piece of the grilled steak and stuck it in her mouth.

The taste was immaculate, and she paused on the salad to put her full attention on the steak.

"That steak good as hell, ain't it?" he asked.

Casey gave him the side eye. "Yea, it's good, but you better watch your mouth," she warned.

"Sorry ma," he apologized.

"Mhm so, again, what's going on?"

"Ain't nothin', really. Just been thinkin' about what's been goin' on these last few months. With Harmony and Brittany. Shit been crazy, to be honest," Chaos stated.

"I'm going to excuse you using profanity because I know that speaking on Harmony is a sensitive subject, but what does Brittany have to do with anything?" she asked.

"She been comin' at me hard about us dealin' again. I just can't see that happenin' again at all."

"Okay, if it won't happen, then why bring her to my home? Why does she have such a mean hold on you, even though you know the truth about that situation?" Casey asked.

Chaos placed his fork down and picked up his orange juice. After he gulped down half of the juice, he placed the glass back down.

"There's no hold on me. I just feel like I'm the only father figure her son had at the time. Although, I don't visit him, I still can't see me just leaving her alone cold turkey. Besides, we just now reconnected; it wasn't like we talked every day. We lost touch for a while and didn't start back talking until the night I got shot, and I brought her here because she popped up at my job wanting to talk. I had no idea Harmony was gonna be here. My main focus was seeing what the hell she wanted, so I didn't even focus on the car that was in the driveway. That was def' my mistake. I would never put Harmony in harm's way or anyone else, for that matter," he explained.

"She came to your job?" Casey asked as she shook her head in disgust. "This is the same problem you had with her back in the day. Brittany is too possessive, and she don't know when to leave well enough alone. Now, you see what she said that night? Only a woman that a man done made comfortable would say such thing. I didn't say anything that night, but Harmony had every right to do what she did. I don't condone violence at the least, but I would have done the same thing if I was Harmony. Understand that Harmony and Brittany are two different women. Don't start back dealing with Brittany, thinking she could fill that empty void that you have now that you're no longer dealing with Harmony."

Chaos listened to every word his mother spoke and he couldn't deny the fact that she was right. He didn't mind going to his mother about his problems or the way he was feeling because he knew she was going to give it to him straight, without sugarcoating a damn thing.

"I feel you, mom, but I'm not tryna get back wit' Brittany or any other woman, for that matter. I'm just tryna focus on the club and gettin' this money. Nothing else really matters," he said, honestly.

Casey took a sip of her orange juice before responding. "Isn't that what got you in this situation in the first place? Chaos, make the money but, baby, don't let it make you or control you."

Casey went back to eating, while Chaos sat there in deep thought. She loved her son dearly, but he was letting his past of struggle define his future, and she didn't like it one bit. She wondered what more would it take for him to know that it was okay to take a break, and she wondered how much longer would it take for him to find out about Kaotic.

Chapter Fourteen

Jasmin & Kaotic Miller:

It was Sunday morning when Kaotic walked in Jasmin's home. He didn't bother knocking because regardless of all the disputes they had going on, he still had a key. Kaotic went into the kitchen, looked into the fridge, and got a Gatorade out. He twisted the cap off and drunk a generous amount, before placing the cap back on and sitting it on the countertop.

"Baby, is that you?" Jasmin called out.

"Yea, come out here!" Kaotic told her.

Jasmin was all smiles when she rushed into the kitchen. She ran over to Kaotic and hugged him tight, as if she hadn't seen him in a while. The only thing she was happy about was the fact that he came over without her having to tell him and, in her eyes, that meant things were getting better between the two.

"Calm down wit' all that mushy shit. You been gettin' shit ready for what I need you to do?" he asked as he pushed her off him.

"Yes, I got the rental like you asked, and I went to Walmart and bought I brand new set of kitchen knives. I went to a different store to get the black gloves you needed. I didn't want to make anything obvious, so I switched it up a little," she told him.

"Good, good," Kaotic said as he rubbed his hands together.

"You never did tell me what this was all about?" Jasmin said in curiosity.

"When shit goes down, you'll know but, in the meantime, I got a little run to make," he said to her before pushing past her and leaving out.

Jasmin was eager to know about what Kaotic was up to; either way, she was going to have his back, and she felt in her heart that helping him handle such a serious situation would finally show him that she was the woman for him.

***

Crystal:

Crystal had just got finished emailing a popular nail tech from Miami about possibly working at her upcoming salon. Since she had left Love and Harmony's boutique months ago, she had been pushing hard to get her nail and hair salon up and running. There had been a few mishaps, but she didn't let that come between her and her dream.

Knock.

Knock.

Knock.

Crystal lived in Indian Run Apartments. It wasn't like her to get company before it just hit noon. It was 11:40 a.m. when she glanced at the time.

"Who is it?" she called out as she walked from the kitchen to the living room.

"A friend of Jasmin's," Kaotic responded.

Crystal was confused because from what she knew, she was Jasmin's only friend at the time before she stopped fucking with her. She unlocked the door and opened it and came face to face with Kaotic. Jasmin talked about Kaotic all the time to Crystal, but she never met him before so she didn't know who he was and, if she did, she would have known to never open the door. Before she could even get a word out, Kaotic grabbed her by her neck and pushed his way inside of her apartment.

"Wha-," Crystal gasped for air as she clawed at his hands.

Bang!

Crash!

Kaotic slammed Crystal into a glass closet that was in her living room. Fear was written all over Crystal's face as she damn near tried fighting for her life.

"Bitch, if you ever in ya life run ya mouth about me, I'ma fuckin' kill you!" Kaotic said before letting go of Crystal's neck.

Cough!

Cough!

Crystal tried to catch her breath and gain heads or tails of the situation. She was completely lost and had no idea who Kaotic was and why he was putting his hands on her.

"Wha-wha-what did I do?" Crystal asked.

"I'm Kaotic. The nigga you been bumpin' ya gums about. Jasmin ain't gon' never leave me alone bitch!" Kaotic barked.

Crystal didn't understand why Kaotic was approaching her over her voicing her opinion months ago. She thought about the way Jasmin left her apartment months back then; this was her way of clapping back at her.

Pussy ass bitch, Crystal thought.

"I have nothing bad to say about you," Crystal said when she was finally about to speak a full sentence.

"Yea, now you don't, but this is ya only warning. The next time I hear you said anything about me tryna get Jasmin to stop fuckin' wit' me. I'ma blow ya fuckin' brains out bitch! Do you understand?" Kaotic threatened.

Crystal nodded yes.

"Nah, speak bitch. Do you understand?" he asked again.

"Yes, I understand," Crystal assured him.

Kaotic gave her a stern look before he walked out. He wanted her to know that, whenever she saw his face, it would be nothing but problems. Crystal felt betrayed by Jasmin. She knew the things she said came off harsh, but she didn't know Jasmin would go as far as she did.

Chapter Fifteen

Chaos Miller:

Knock. Knock.

Knock.

Casey was making herself a cup of coffee when she heard a knock at the door. She was only expecting one person and she prayed it was them and not Kaotic. She still had unfinished business with him, and she knew she still had to figure out how to come clean to Chaos about the secrets she kept.

"Thank God, it's you and not someone else," Casey exclaimed when she opened the door.

She welcomed Brittany in as she sipped her freshly brewed coffee. Brittany was still very beautiful after all these years and, for her to be in her thirties, she didn't look a day over twenty-five. Brittany stood at five-foot-eight-inches with the *body measurements of 33-24-35, and she had a beautiful caramel complexion. Her reddish burgundy hair was cut in a nice bob, and she was always dressed nice from head to toe.*

Brittany reminded Casey of Harmony, only because of her boss like ways. She loved a woman about her business, and taking care of business was something both Harmony and Brittany was good at.

"How are you doing Casey?" Brittany asked.

"I'm blessed sweetie. Would you like a cup of coffee? It's fresh," Casey said.

"Oh, that would be lovely. Do you mind if I sit down?" Brittany asked.

"Not at all," Casey said as she placed her cup of coffee on the countertop and began to fix Brittany a cup.

It took her all but a few minutes and, once she was done, she grabbed both cups and shimmied her way to the kitchen table.

"So, what's going on my mother from another?" Brittany asked and then took a sip of her coffee, leaving a faint lipstick stain on the rim of the cup.

"The question is, what is going on with you? Don't act like I forgot about the altercation missy," Casey said with a raised eyebrow.

Brittany gave a slight chuckle before she spoke. "I had no intentions for it to even turn physical, but Harmony definitely has some issues she's dealing with herself, and she got all in her feelings because I stopped by to see my friend."

"Brittany, that is her husband and she is my daughter-in-law, and I can understand her frustration. She had no clue that you and Chaos were friends, and you honestly just popped up out of the blue," Casey said.

Brittany took another sip of coffee. "Chaos didn't seem bothered either time I called, so I popped up. Why are you upset with me and not your son?" she asked.

"I'm not upset, but you have crossed a line of respect that should not have been crossed. Granted, you and my son have a past, but he is married now. I had no idea that you and him were trying to rekindle an old flame," Casey stated.

"Chaos isn't trying to rekindle anything with me. Do I miss him? Yes, I do, and I understand he has a wife, but Chaos also has a responsibility that he has yet to take part in," Brittany shot back.

Casey shook her head back and forth.

"A responsibility that you and him both agreed that he didn't need to be there. This was way before Harmony and it should stay that way. Chaos was in the streets bad back then and he made a few mistakes. I have a lot of love for you, Brittany. You are a sweet girl, but you cannot try to sabotage that man's marriage because you made a decision that you regret now. You were a young girl and you were dealing with a popular boy and you did what all young girls did. The decision you made is something you had and will continue to live with."

Casey had respect for Brittany on the strength of her being down for Chaos when he was in the streets. However, she was a woman and she could see right through Brittany's sneaky ways.

"With all due respect, Casey. The situation between me and Chaos is just that. I love him and I always have, and me being his friend shouldn't be a problem. His wife needs to just be confident enough because now that I'm back in his life, I don't plan on leaving it again," Brittany's response was bold and confident.

She had lost ties with Chaos once and she had no plans on doing so again. She was well aware that Harmony and Chaos were together, but the bond that she and Chaos shared was undeniable. Brittany was his rider and she wasn't going to allow Harmony to take what was hers to begin with.

"You're barking up the wrong tree Brittany. My son is happy and he is no longer Chaos from the streets. He has a legitimate business and he is doing things the legal way. Don't try and turn him back to the streets because they don't love him, his family does," Casey's tone was firm and motherlike.

Brittany took a few more sips of her coffee and then reached for her purse. She opened it and reached inside and pulled out some pictures.

"This," she pointed at the pictures, "is his family, okay? I've been playing the back seat for the last six years and, frankly, I'm tired of it. I was Chaos' rock when he was in the streets, and I'll be damned if he forgets it. Casey, you may not like that I'm back in the picture, but you have no choice but to respect it. At one point, you loved seeing my face. I used to come to your house all the time and now things have changed? You act as if I'm some stranger when, in all reality, I'm way more than that."

"Things have changed because Chaos has moved on and he's married now. I'm not sure what you're not understanding, but you will not bring up the past to keep a hold on my son. Whatever tricks you have up your sleeve can stay right there. I understand you held him down a few times while he was in the streets but, baby, whether you like it or not, Harmony was there a lot more than you. She kept him sane and she got him out of those streets, something I prayed for many of nights," Casey paused and placed her hand on top of Brittany's. "Baby, sometimes a man is setting himself up to be a better man for another woman. Chaos was a certain type of man when he was with you, but he became another type of man when he got with Harmony, and I love the man my son is with her."

Casey may have been old, but her husband was in the streets as well and she knew what it was like to be a down ass bitch to a thug ass nigga. She was trying her hardest to set Brittany straight in a reasonable manner, but she was a tough cookie to break.

Brittany stood up because the tension was getting thick in the room and she knew that Chaos would never forgive her for snatching his mother up and dragging her all across that kitchen floor.

"I can see that our time here is done." Brittany grabbed the pictures and put them back in her purse. "Chaos is and always has been my first love. I can't just forget about that, no matter who likes it or not. Thanks for the coffee."

Brittany pushed her chair in and proceeded to head for the door.

"Brittany, just let it go. It's one thing to be a down ass bitch, but it's another thing to be a wife."

The words that Casey spoke hit Brittany like a ton of bricks. It took everything in her not to turn around and leap on Casey, but she took the high road and walked out of her house. She unlocked her car and got in while throwing her purse in the passenger side seat. Brittany didn't understand why Chaos never chose her to be his wife but, even if it was the last thing she would do, she was damn sure going to find out.

"Why you so quiet?" he asked.

It was Tuesday, the fourth of July, and both Chaos and Brittany were out enjoying a good meal at Long Horn Steak House before they caught the fireworks. Chaos nor Brittany were dating, but it felt good for him to be out getting some fresh air.

"I'm just thinking. That's all," Brittany responded.

"The fuck you thinkin' about that got you quiet for most of the damn dinner?" Chaos asked.

He was in no mood for any bullshit from Brittany or from any woman period, so his words were straight up and to the point.

"Calm down, damn. I was just thinking about the conversation me and your mother had a few months back, that's all."

"Conversation? About what? Because whatever it was must've been some shit because you still thinkin' about it but, then again, my mother's words have that effect on people, so what she say?" Chaos asked.

"Basically telling me how I need to just leave you alone and move on with my life because you're a married man," Brittany told him.

Chaos cleared his throat. "Ya arm healed up nice," he tried changing the subject.

"Her words really hurt me, Chaos. I love your mother as if she was my own. I would come by the house all the time when we were dealing. What changed?" she asked.

"Brittany, why do you keep doin' this to yaself? What we had in the past is just that," he said.

"Really? So, you don't have any feelings left for me? If that's the case, then why are we at dinner right now? Why do you keep leading me on?" she asked.

"Leadin' you on?" Chaos frowned. "Brittany, ain't nobody been leadin' you on. Just because I'm an ear when you need it don't mean anything, and I was hungry and you hit me up right before I was about to step out, that's why we're at dinner. Why you tryna make this more than what it is?" Chaos asked.

"Because I love you, Chaos, and I miss you. I want it to be an us again. I miss you coming over late lights and us fucking until the sun came up. It's been six years too long and I just don't know how much longer I can go on without having you to myself," she spoke honestly.

Chaos was in no mood for Brittany's feelings. He knew the night he responded to her text was a bad idea, but he did it anyway against his better judgement.

"I can't even go there wit' you again ma," Chaos kept it real with Brittany time and time again, but it just wasn't enough.

"You can't go there with me? Why not? Are you and Harmony ever going to get back together? I think not because if you were, then yawl would be together now. She must have did something real fucked up for yawl to take such a long ass break," Brittany shot back.

Chaos chuckled. He knew Brittany was trying to do whatever she could to get him to agree with being with her, but it wasn't going to happen. He always knew that she was trying to get some dirt on Harmony so she could say *I told you so*, but he would never give her the satisfaction.

"That's exactly why we'll never be together. Now, can we enjoy our meal? I'm tryna get up outta here soon," Chaos said, cutting the conversation short.

Brittany poked her lips out and sat back in her seat. She was beyond frustrated, but she wasn't going to stop until she had Chaos back in her grasp.

Chapter Sixteen

Harmony Winfield-Miller:

Harmony tossed and turned all night. She could barely eat or sleep for the past two weeks. What Kaotic told her was eating at her, and what made it so bad was the fact that as bad as she wanted to tell Chaos, he wouldn't give her the time of day. If it wasn't concerning her boutique, the house, or the bills, Chaos did not want to talk to her. It had been exactly four months since they had been separated and it felt like years to Harmony.

She took Renee's advice and tried her hardest to get Chaos' attention so that she could tell him, but he wasn't budging and she honestly couldn't blame him. Although the information she knew had been told to her months ago, it seemed to eat at her more because she couldn't do anything about it. She didn't know who to go to or what to do.

After speaking with Casey, she'd figured maybe Chaos would come to her about his mother finally telling him the truth about Kaotic but, knowing Casey, she was too afraid to say anything because Chaos had already been through enough.

Just then, an idea hit her and she figured since Chaos wouldn't listen to her, then her best bet was to go to the ones closest to him, and that was Brave and Coroner. She knew that things could go real left or real right but, either way, she needed to tell the truth and tell it fast or things were going to spiral out of control once again, and someone could even lose their life this time and she couldn't have that on her conscious.

She picked up her cellphone and scrolled through her contacts until she came across Brave's number. After pressing the call button, she listened to the phone ring and was praying he didn't send her to voicemail.

Ringgg. Ringgg.

Ringgg.

"Please answer, please answer," Harmony prayed.

Ringgg.

Ringgg.

"Yo?" Brave asked and then cleared his throat.

"Hello? Brave? Are you busy?" she asked.

Brave looked at his phone and then sat up in his bed.

"Busy? A nigga sleep Harmony, what the fuck you doin' callin' a nigga and wakin' him up? What do you want girl?" Brave snapped.

"I'm sorry. I thought you would've been at the club," she apologized.

"Nah, Chaos been closing early on certain days, so I brung my black ass home and went to sleep. Wassup tho? You good?" he asked.

It took Harmony a minute to respond because she didn't like the fact that Chaos waited until they were over to start closing the club down on certain days. All she wanted was his time and attention, and it seemed like it was still going to everyone but her.

"Harmony, you good?" Brave asked again.

"I'm sorry Brave but, no, I'm not," she stated honestly.

"What's wrong?" Brave asked in a serious tone.

"I need you to get Coroner and come over here. I have something to tell yawl. I tried to tell Chaos, but he won't unblock me and he won't respond to my texts once I let him know that it doesn't concern the house, the bills or the boutique," she explained.

Brave didn't say another word. He hopped out of the bed and put on the same clothes he had on yesterday. He didn't bother to brush his teeth or wash his face. Brave put on his Timberland boots, grabbed his gun, and was out the door before Harmony could say another word.

Chapter Seventeen

Harmony Winfield-Miller, Brave & Coroner:

The wee hours of Wednesday morning, and Brave and Coroner made it to Harmony and Chaos' house simultaneously.

"What's goin' on?" Coroner asked when he got out of his car.

"I don't know, but sis called me sayin' she needed me, so I know somethin' is up," Brave said as they both walked to the door.

Knock.

Knock.

Harmony was sitting on the couch when she heard the knock at the door. She knew it had to be Brave, so she quickly got up and hurried to the door.

"Thank you for coming," she said when she opened the door and let them both in.

"No problem. What's goin' on?" Brave asked.

"Come sit down because yawl gonna need to take a seat when I tell yawl this," she said.

Brave didn't like the feeling he was getting. He was hoping Harmony didn't get herself caught up in some more bullshit.

"Just let me know what the hell is goin' on sis because you know a nigga like me ain't about no games," Brave said, wanting her to cut straight to the chase.

"Yea boss lady. Let us know what's going on. Don't hold anything back," Coroner chimed in.

Harmony took a deep breath. She was nervous to speak, but she knew she had to. There was no other way for her to get the truth out, and now was her chance.

"I know who shot Chaos," she blurted.

"Who?" Brave asked.

"His brother," she revealed.

Brave and Coroner both looked at each other. The word brother threw them both off.

"Brother? Chaos ain't got no brother," Brave said.

"That's what I thought but, apparently, Casey has been keeping some secrets away from Chaos and that was one of them," Harmony said.

"How the fuck do you know this Harmony? Don't tell me you was in on this shit because if so, you already know how shit gon' end for you," Brave warned her.

He didn't care how Harmony felt about the threat he made. They all knew that, if Harmony had anything to do with what happened to Chaos, she was just as dead as the nigga who shot him, and that was one time where Chaos wasn't going to hesitate on pulling the trigger.

"No! I had nothing to do with it. I just made a stupid mistake. The guy I cheated on Chaos with was his brother, and I didn't know until he came to my boutique and choked me!" Harmony cried.

"The nigga put his hands on you?" Brave asked.

"You cheated on Chaos?" Coroner asked in shock.

Harmony was in tears. It made her sick to her stomach to admit the truth. She didn't care about how it made her look; all she cared about was letting them know everything she knew.

"Fuck all that Coroner. This nigga put his hands on you?" Brave asked again.

"Yes, I wanted to tell Chaos, but he won't talk to me. I can understand he's upset, but I need him to know the truth since Casey won't tell him. I even plan on getting an abortion, since I don't know who my child's father is," Harmony told them.

"This shit is crazy." Brave shook his head.

Harmony had fucked up big time, but the blame was no longer on her. Brave couldn't believe that Casey held back on telling Chaos he had a brother. That didn't seem like her but, the way he grew up, he didn't put anything past anyone.

"We gotta tell Chaos about this. We need to dead this nigga and dead this nigga fast. As far as Casey, Chaos gotta handle that and, sis, as far as that baby, you need to get rid of that. Even if it's a possibility of it being Chaos' baby, yawl gotta take that L and try again because we can't take no chances. But, as of right now, give me and Coroner a day to get Chaos in the right mind so that he can talk to you," Brave told her.

Harmony didn't protest. She agreed with every word Brave spoke. Months had gone by and she was just now showing. She didn't speak of the baby or wear clothes that were revealing. Harmony knew that she would probably suffer later down the line, but she just didn't give two fucks about the life that was growing inside of her.

Chapter Eighteen

Kaotic Miller & Casey Miller:

11:30 p.m. Friday night, Kaotic sat a house down from Casey's house. He had given Casey numerous chances to be honest and upfront with Chaos, but he knew like the coward she was that she wasn't going to tell the truth, and that was okay with him.

"Pull up a little," Kaotic told Jasmin as he put on the black gloves she had purchased for him.

"Whose house is this?" she asked.

"Don't worry about that. Just keep the car started," Kaotic ordered before getting out of the car.

He reached in his hoodie and held onto the stainless-steel kitchen knife. Kaotic had a mean grip on it as he walked up the mini ramp and knocked on the door.

Knock. Knock.
Knock.

Kaotic was smart. He chose a day that he knew Chaos wouldn't be able to come to Casey's rescue because he would be working. He was well aware that the club was busy on the weekends.

"Chaos, you better start using your key," Casey said from the other side as she unlocked the door.

The moment she opened the door, Kaotic pulled the knife out of his hoodie pocket and plunged it in her stomach. Casey couldn't get a word out as a shocking look came across her eyes. Kaotic pushed himself inside as he stabbed Casey in the stomach repeatedly. Blood gushed from Casey's mouth, but that didn't stop Kaotic from constantly stabbing her.

"Dumb bitch! All you had to do was be honest and this would have never happened!" he cursed as he continued to stab her.

Several minutes passed, and Kaotic's face was drenched in sweat. Casey had collapsed on the floor in a pool of blood. He stuck the knife back in his hoodie and then turned to walk back to the door. Kaotic made sure he didn't step in any blood. He wanted Chaos to know that he was the one that murdered their mother, but he didn't want it to be an easy task for him. He put the knife back inside of his hood pocket, took the gloves off before turning off the kitchen light, and closed the door behind him. Kaotic jogged back to the car and got in.

"A'ight, let's go," he told Jasmin in a calm tone.

Jasmin pulled off. She could tell that whatever went down in that house wasn't good because Kaotic was sweating and he had taken the gloves off.

"Back to my place?" Jasmin asked.

"Nah, drop me off in Fairton. But, I'm a leave the knife and glove wrapped up in the hoodie. Take it and throw it in the Cohansey River when you make it back to Bridgeton after dropping me off, okay?"

"Okay, I love you, Kaotic. I just want you to know that," Jasmin said as she turned her attention back on the road.

Kaotic ignored her. He didn't want or care about her love. The only woman he knew for a fact that had any sort of love or care for him was Boots, and he would never forget the things she's done.

Kaotic Miller & Boots:

"Don't forget to come by later!" Jasmin called out as she pulled off.

Kaotic waved her off and walked up to Boots' door. It had been a long time since he even made contact with her again, and he knew she was going to be pissed. They didn't end on good terms, and now was the best time to try and make things right.

Knock. Knock.

Knock.

Kaotic knocked hard three times, enough for Boots to get up at a fast pace and, just like he suspected, he heard moving around in the house. He heard footsteps and then fumbling with the door before she appeared from the other side.

"What are you doing here?" she asked in a raspy tone.

Boots already knew it was Kaotic because she looked through the peephole. She hadn't seen him in months, but that was to be suspected.

"I need to talk to you. Can I come in?" Kaotic asked.

Boots never denied him, as much as she wanted to. No matter how much she tried to be done with him, the love she had for him always overpowered her.

"What's going on?" she asked when she closed the door behind him. They walked down the hall and into her living room to take a seat.

"I killed her. I killed that bitch and it felt damn good," Kaotic admitted.

Boots rubbed the sleep out of her eyes and looked at Kaotic in disbelief. "Killed who Kaotic? Please don't tell me you are talking about your mother?" she asked.

A big smile spread across his face as he nodded his head up and down.

"Hell yea. I feel so good baby, and I feel like I can finally be okay now. I feel like I can give you my heart without feeling like I'll be a dumbass if I give my heart to another woman," he said.

Boots couldn't believe what she was hearing. She knew Kaotic was crazy, but right then let her know how insane he really was and she wanted no parts of it.

"Kaotic, you killed your mother? How could you do something like that?" she asked.

"I had to. The bitch wouldn't tell the truth, so I killed her. I feel better now Boots; ain't that what you always wanted? You wanted me to heal, and I am; I'm healed now girl, now stop playin' wit' me." Kaotic tried to pull Boots close to him, but she pulled away.

"Kaotic, stop. You killed your mother. That's not something I wanted." She pushed him back. "I think you need to leave. I just need time to think about all of this."

"Leave? What the fuck you mean leave? I came all the way over here to make shit right wit' you and you want me to leave?" his tone of voice became angry.

"No, it's not that. I just need some time to think, that's all," Boots lied.

She could hear the anger in his voice and the last thing she wanted to do was become one of his next victims.

"Oh, I was about to say man don't do me like that because it took a lot for me to even come here and say this shit. I'ma give you some time, but don't try to play me, Boots fareal. I swear on everything, I will kill you; you know how I am when it comes to my heart. It done been stepped on one too many times by the woman that was supposed to be my mother and look how she ended up," Kaotic said.

"I understand and, no, I'm not tryna play with you. I just need some time Kaotic because all of this is just an all of a sudden thing. We didn't end on good terms last time and I truly thought we were done. All I need is a couple days to just think things through, but I also want you to lay low because this shit is serious and how are we going to be together if you go to prison?" she asked.

Boots was doing everything in her power to get Kaotic to remain comfortable. She didn't want him to feel uneasy, so she did all that she could to make him feel like everything was good. Her main focus was getting him out of her house and locking the door behind him.

"I feel you but, damn, I got dropped off here. I ain't even got my car," he told her.

Boots quickly grabbed the keys off her coffee table. "Take my car. This way, you'll know that we will be seeing each other again." She forced a fake laugh.

"Damn girl," he said as he took the keys then kissed her. "You must be tryna really get rid of a nigga."

Boots rolled her eyes. "That's not it Kay. For one, I want to go back to sleep and, for two, you just did some crazy shit and you don't need to be out. You need to be somewhere laying low and my house is not the place. You know what I do for a living and I always have the state coming back and forth to my house. I don't need you being seen dummy."

"You right, ma bad. I'm not laying too low. I'm a be chillin' at ma crib like I been doin'. Ain't nobody gon' come lookin' for me. They don't want them problems, but just hit me when you ready to talk," he said and then got up.

Boots got up off the couch as well. She walked him down the hallway to the door and opened it.

"Be safe, and don't mess up ma car boy." Boots playfully pushed him out the door.

Kaotic chuckled and walked to her car. Boots didn't even wait to see if he got in before closing the door and locking it. She was scared shitless, but she was thankful he was out of her house. When she heard the car start up and saw the lights pulling out of her driveway, she rushed to her computer and sat down. After pulling up Kaotic's documents, she pulled Chaos' documents right along with it and managed to get his contact number. Boots knew that Kaotic was dead serious when he told her that he killed Casey and, considering she was the one that gave out her information, she felt like it was only right that she made the call.

Chapter Nineteen

Chaos Miller, Harmony Winfield-Miller, Brave, Renee & Coroner:

Chaos' heart was shattered into pieces when he got the call that Casey had been killed. At first, he didn't believe it but, when he got to his mother's house and saw the EMT's bringing a body out in a black bag, he flipped out. He couldn't believe that his last living parent had been taken away from him in a blink of an eye.

"Bruh, just listen to what she gotta say. I know you hurtin' right now. I know. Casey was like a mother to me as well, so her death is just as fucked up to me as it is to you, but Harmony got some shit to tell you bruh, some serious shit to tell you, and I need you to listen to what the fuck she gotta say. I would have just went ahead and handled this shit for you, but I felt like this shit was more personal than ever," Brave explained.

"I don't wanna hear shit she got to say. I don't even know why the fuck you invited her over. My muthafuckin' mother just got killed and all you can tell me is to listen to what the fuck Harmony gotta say?" Chaos looked at Brave with hate in his eyes.

Brave couldn't blame Chaos for the way he was feeling, but now was not the time to be against one another. They all had to put their focus on one person and one person only.

"Boss man, please, just hear her out when she gets here, please," Coroner chimed in.

"Real talk, bruh. I wouldn't lead you onto no bullshit. If you want the nigga who shot you and killed mommy. Listen to what Harmony has to say when she gets here," Brave said.

Chaos was now interested. He winced a little at the mention of his mother because death and her in the same sentence just didn't sound right to him. Boots didn't tell Chaos that Kaotic was his brother. She made up a story so that it didn't sound like she was involved. She acted like a concerned neighbor and called the police when she heard loud noises coming from next door.

They were all at Brave's house when Harmony saw car lights outside of the house. Brave got up and went to the door and opened it. He was met by Harmony and Renee. The moment Harmony saw Chaos, she rushed over to hug him, but he pushed her.

"Don't fuckin' touch me," he spat.

Brave had already let Harmony know about what happened to Casey so that she would be on point if Chaos snapped.

"Chaos, please don't do this. Baby, I know you're hurting, but don't fight me right now. We need to come together right now," she cried.

"I don't got time for this shit. Yo, if she don't say what the fuck she gotta say, I'm outta here," Chaos said while looking at Brave.

He was doing everything he could to fight back the tears that was trying to force their way out. Chaos wanted to accept Harmony's love, but the anger and hurt in him wouldn't allow it.

"Harmony, just let him know what you know," Brave said calmly.

Harmony's eyes were blood shot red from crying. Within the last few months, her life had fell completely apart. She blamed everything on herself and she prayed that, by telling Chaos the truth, it would make up for all the pain she'd caused him.

"Chaos, you have a brother. His name is Kaotic and Casey gave him up for adoption. She couldn't take care of both of yawl, so she gave him up instead of you. Kaotic is also the same guy I had an affair with. I didn't know yawl were brothers and that he was the same guy that shot you until he came to the boutique one day and told me. When I tried to call the police, he choked me and I was scared. He knew that you wouldn't listen to me because of all that I had done, so I went to Casey and she said she knew about Kaotic shooting you. She was just scared to tell you and-"

In the midst of her explaining everything she knew, Harmony broke down in tears as she looked at Chaos. He was standing in Brave's living room with his hands in his pockets, with a blank look. Harmony knew he was hurting and she hated the fact that she couldn't do anything about it.

"Bro, I know you hurtin' right now, but sis is tellin' the truth. This ain't no funny shit to try and get back in good graces with you. This here is the real deal and we need to get this nigga as soon as possible," Brave told him.

Silent tears rolled down Chaos' face as he nodded his head. He took his right hand out of his pocket and wiped his face without saying a word. Chaos knew Harmony wasn't lying. He could see the sincerity in her face and hear it in her voice. His mother was dead and gone, but killing the nigga who did it would bring justice for his mother and allow her to rest in peace.

"Where that nigga live at?" he asked, looking directly at Harmony.

Brave knew what time it was and, when that old Chaos came out, there was nothing that could stop him.

Chapter Twenty

Harmony Winfield-Miller & Kaotic Miller:

Kaotic was relaxing in his recliner while watching tv, when his phone went off. He was already in the process of texting Jasmin's annoying ass, when he saw Harmony's name pop up in his text messages.

Harmony: *Hey, I know it's been a while since we talked, but I have to talk to you. I was pissed when you came to my boutique telling me all that you told me but, the reality is, I fucked up. I'm pregnant and I can bet my life on it that you're the father. I'm scared Kaotic. I don't know what it's like to be a mother. My own damn mother wasn't in my life. I want my child to have a family and, if this baby isn't something you want, the*

least you can do is go to the abortion clinic with me.

Kaotic read her text. He laughed at how stressed Harmony was, and it made him feel good because he knew she would come running back because there was no way Chaos was going to want her again. Things always worked out in his favor and, if responding to her text would allow him the chance to fuck Harmony again, he was all for it.

Kaotic: *I knew you would come crawlin' back. You know the address. We'll talk about all that baby shit when you get here.*

Harmony showed Chaos the text when Kaotic wrote back. He nodded his head, and she watched as Chaos, Brave, and Coroner loaded up their guns.

"Coroner, we gon' take ya truck. As for you, you gon' have to make things seem as normal as possible. This nigga said you know the address, so pull up in ya own whip. We gon be parked down the street. The moment you make it in the house, make sure that nigga don't lock the door. Whatever room is in the front keep him there, you got it?" Chaos asked after he explained the game plan to her.

"Yes, I got it," she assured.

Harmony: *Okay, I'll be there after I shower.*

Harmony text Kaotic back to buy them some time until the sun went down. She knew that shit was going to get real, but her loyalty lied with Chaos; no matter how many times she fucked Kaotic, her heart and her loyalty was with her husband.

***

Kaotic Miller & Harmony Winfield-Miller:

It was just hitting 8 p.m. when Harmony pulled in Kaotic's driveway. Her stomach was doing back flips, but knowing that Chaos was about to put an end to Kaotic once and for all made her calm down a little. She pulled down her visor and looked in the mirror to apply a little bit of lip gloss. She didn't want to put on any makeup because she wanted Kaotic to see that she was really stressed.

Harmony: *I'm outside.*

Harmony had to play it off, if she wanted everything to run smoothly. She put the car in park, got out, and slammed the door behind her. She walked up to his door, and he opened it with a smirk on his face.

"I see you made sure you was lookin' good for a nigga," he said as he admired Harmony in her all-black sundress.

It hugged her body tight and even showed her pregnant belly that grew out of nowhere.

"I didn't want to come over here looking busted. I know I'm stressed, but I don't have to look it, do I?"

"I feel you," Kaotic said as he welcomed her in.

When Harmony walked in, she turned to Kaotic and kissed him and then pulled away quickly.

"I'm sorry. I just missed you, and I couldn't help myself," she apologized before closing the door.

"I knew you missed me. Once I put this dick in you, I knew you was gon' be around regardless. You might as well take that dress off because I'm about to drop this dick off in you. Like I said, we can talk about that baby shit later," Kaotic said.

Bang!

Whap!

Whap! Smack!

Pop! Bang!

Chaos had kicked in the door, with Brave and Coroner right on his heels. He smashed Kaotic in his face with his gun the moment he saw him. Harmony made sure she got out of the way, as she watched all three men beat Kaotic to a bloody pulp.

"Bitch, you set me up," he slurred and then spit his teeth on the floor.

"You damn right I set you up nigga," she boasted.

Kaotic managed to laugh, even with his bloody and swollen mouth.

"Go head and kill me. I don't give a fuck," he said with confidence.

Chaos wanted to make him suffer, just like he knew his mother suffered. He nodded his head towards Coroner, who kneeled and wrapped his big, meaty arm around Kaotic's neck and squeeze tight. Kaotic began to gasp for air, and that was exactly what Chaos wanted him to do. As he gasped for air and just moments before Coroner was about to snap his neck, he let him go and stood up.

Boc! Boc! Boc!

Boc! Boc! Boc!

Boc! Boc! Boc

REDS JOHNSON

Chaos and Brave riddled Kaotic's body with bullets, as he laid there lifeless on his living room floor. Chaos didn't give a fuck about Kaotic being his brother or not; he had violated to no return, so he had to get dealt with. Harmony had never witnessed Chaos kill someone before, so she was scared to death when she looked at him and she didn't see her husband. He looked at her with his gun still in his hand and, just as she was about to speak, Chaos stopped her.

"Go get in the car," he said.

Harmony didn't say anything in return; she just went along and did as she was told. She left out of Kaotic's house, ran to her car, and got in.

"Boss, go home. I'll have this cleaned up in no time," Coroner assured Chaos and Brave.

Chaos gave him a nod and left out with Brave right behind him. They both walked over to Harmony's car and got in. Harmony wanted to say something to Chaos, but she knew now just wasn't the time. She stuck her key in the ignition, started the car, put it in reverse, and pulled out of the driveway. She then put the car in drive and pulled off without looking back. Kaotic was just a memory, and he was

238

one memory that she never wanted to remember ever again.

Chapter Twenty-One

Chaos Miller, Harmony Winfield-Miller & Brave:

"Bro, I'ma stay the night and just go home in the am," Brave said when they pulled up to Harmony and Chaos' home.

He wanted to make sure Chaos wasn't going to do anything crazy, so staying the night would give him the chance to keep an eye on him.

"That's cool," Chaos said dryly.

Harmony didn't intervene. They all got out of the car and headed into the house. Harmony hurried upstairs to get Brave a blanket and a pillow. Brave knew he could sleep in one of the guest rooms, but he liked to be in the living room where he could hear everything and be the first one to pop if something were to kick off.

"Thanks sis," Brave said when Harmony gave him the blanket and pillow.

She waited until Chaos disappeared upstairs before responding to Brave.

"No, thank you," she said.

"For what?" he asked.

"For being there for me and listening to me, even though I messed up."

"That ain't about nothin' sis. Just gotta be smarter next time. Now, go get some sleep," he told her.

Harmony nodded her head in agreement and then walked up the stairs. She could hear the shower running when she entered the bedroom. Harmony sat on the bed and waited for Chaos to come out. It had been so long since he had stepped foot in their bedroom, let alone take a shower there. She prayed that they could come to some sort of common ground and possibly work on their marriage.

Several minutes later, Chaos came out of the bathroom with a towel wrapped around his waist. Harmony wanted to make sweet, passionate love to Chaos right then and there, but she knew that was the least thing on his mind.

"Chaos, can we talk?" she asked.

He sighed as he sat on the edge of the bed and then wiped his hands down his face.

"About what Harmony?" he asked in an uninterested tone. "What could you possibly want to talk about? My mother is dead, I killed my brother that I met for the first time, and my wife is pregnant by God knows who. Please enlighten me on what you wanna talk about?"

Chaos made Harmony feel like a piece of shit at that moment. She knew things were bad but, when she really heard it verbally, it just made everything far much worse.

"I'm sorry Chaos. For everything. I know I fucked up and you probably will never forgive me but, baby, I never stopped loving you. I just wanted your time and attention and it seemed like you gave it to everyone else but me. I never meant to hurt or betray you. What happened, just happened out of nowhere. I enjoyed the time and attention he gave me. I felt so alive and so loved, and that's all I ever wanted from you. Turns out that he seeked me out, just to get back at you."

Chaos chuckled. He spoke to Harmony with his back still turned, without even looking at her.

"You cheated on me for a fuck boy ass nigga that fucked you to get back at me? He didn't even really want you. You violated me and what we had for a good time and got played in the process. You was just a pawn in his game of chess ma."

Harmony couldn't argue with him because he was speaking the truth. As bad as it sounded, she was thankful that Chaos was even having a conversation with her, so she was going to take all the blows he threw at her.

"You're right, and all I can do is apologize to you, Chaos. I miss you so much baby, and I'm willing to do any and everything for you to take me back. Life without you is so fucked up," she confessed.

"When you had me, you didn't want me. What's gon' make things different now?" he asked.

"Patience, baby, and understanding. I understand you have a business, but just don't forget about me in the process."

Chaos thought long and hard. He couldn't front and act like he didn't miss Harmony because he did, but it was going to take a long time to rebuild the trust that was broken.

"It's gon' take some time Harmony. Just because that nigga dead don't mean you can snap ya fingers and shit gon' be back to normal just like that. You still pregnant, and it's a strong possibility that you carryin' his baby because we ain't fucked in a long ass time."

"I'll get an abortion," Harmony blurted. "I already planned on doing so. I want you back Chaos and I'm not joking about that."

Chaos knew that Harmony loved him, and the fact that she was willing to kill an unborn child just so he could take her back proved a lot. He wasn't happy about any of the events that took place, but he couldn't control certain things life handed him. It was going to take Chaos a long time to heal from what Harmony did to him and heal from his mother's death but, with time, anything was possible.

"We gotta start off slow and work our way back up. I'm not moving back in right away. I'll be staying at Brave's place until I feel like I'm ready to come back. That's all I can give you right now," he told her.

Harmony's heart almost jumped out of her chest. She was so excited to hear those words come out of Chaos' mouth that she hopped off the bed, walked in front of him, wrapped her arms around his neck, and hugged him tight.

"I accept that. Just as long as I know that, in due time, we will be back together. I love you so much, Chaos."

Chaos slowly wrapped his arms around Harmony's waist and it felt good. He needed to feel that love and affection after everything that had gone on.

"I love you too, Harmony."

Chapter Twenty-Two

Chaos Miller & Mahogany:

Monday, the morning of his mother's burial, Chaos decided to make a long-awaited trip. He had shed so many tears before and after the service that he was actually strong enough to do what it was that he was about to do. It took Chaos about twenty-five minutes to get to Bridgeton.

He pulled onto the street that brought him back plenty of aggravating memories but, at this point, all he could was laugh it off. Chaos pulled into the driveway off the one-story family home. It had been years since he been there, but today being the day he finished his unfinished business from years ago.

Chaos parked, shut the car off, and got out. He walked up the walk way, then the porch, and knocked on the door.

Knock. Knock.

Knock.

He waited for a few moments and then attempted to knock again, but the door slung open.

"What the hell are you doing here?"

Chaos bit his tongue, as usual. "It's nice to see you again, Mahogany. Is it okay if I come in and talk? It's very important," he said.

Mahogany, who was Harmony's mother, hated Chaos' guts. She didn't want her daughter with a thug like him and she did everything she could to keep them apart, but it didn't work.

"I got a little bit of free time. Come on in, but don't think you staying long," she said with an attitude.

"It's cool. A few minutes is all I need," he told her as he walked in.

Mahogany closed the door behind him and walked past him. "Come in the living room," she demanded.

Chaos followed her into the living room and took a seat on the recliner in the corner.

"Now, what is there to talk about? You got my daughter pregnant? Or you cheating on her? Which one is it?" she asked.

Chaos put his head down and laughed as he shook his head back and forth. "You always been a piece of work, but no, Harmony isn't pregnant nor am I cheating on her," Chaos shut her accusations down.

"Hmmm." Mahogany sat back on the couch, rolled her eyes, and folded her arms across her chest.

"Look, with all due respect Mahogany, for as long as I've known you, you have always been disrespectful to me and not once have I been disrespectful to you. I came here today to tell you life is too short. I just lost my mother, and here you are not even wanting to be a mother. All because you didn't want your daughter with me. Well, I'm not going anywhere anytime soon, and you need to just get used to it. Harmony is hurting without you and she's been hurting without you. My mother tried to help but, now, she's gone so nobody can fill that void but you now. Maybe if you wasn't so angry at her father, then you could actually be a good mother. This don't make no damn sense and, to be real, yawl both stubborn, but you should know better." Chaos shook his head at her and got up. "If you even get the courage to be a mother, Harmony's number is still the same."

Chaos walked out of the living room and headed to the door. He let himself out and left Mahogany there to sulk in her own misery, which was exactly what she did because as soon as he walked out, she broke down crying as she thought about the last time she spoke to her daughter.

Harmony had just got finished getting dressed. Her outfit was simple but cute. She had on a white v-neck shirt and a pair of black biker shorts, along with her all-white Nikes. She grabbed her overnight bag that she had purchased a few weeks ago and headed downstairs.

"Mom, I'm about to leave," she spoke as she continued to walk, hoping her mother wouldn't give her any problems. But, as always, Harmony counted her chickens before they could hatch and ended up being disappointed.

"I beg your pardon young lady? You ain't going nowhere. I told you before I didn't want you hanging with that no-good thug and I meant it." Mahogany gave her daughter a quick glance before continuing to fix dinner.

Harmony stopped in her tracks. She could feel her blood boil by her mother's response, so she took a deep breath.

"What do you mean I'm not going anywhere? Chaos is my boyfriend and last time I checked, I was grown," Harmony sassed.

She was twenty-one years old at the time but, in her mother's eyes, she still had Similac on her tongue.

"Little girl, I know you better watch who you talking to. Because if yo ass was so grown, then you wouldn't be living under my roof! And you gon' abide by my rules, as long as yo ass is here. If you want to be with that no-good son of a bitch, then get yo shit and get out! But, I refuse to see my daughter go downhill while she's living with me."

It seemed as though Mahogany was waiting for this moment because she said a mouth full. She paused on dinner and turned away from the stove as she folded her arms across her chest, waiting for her daughters' response.

Harmony was taken aback by her mother's choice of words. She didn't like when he spoke about

Chaos in a nasty way because he wasn't the man she portrayed him to be.

"Watch your mouth when you mention Chaos, mom. He isn't here to defend himself and I'm not gon' let you talk about him as if he's this terrible person, because he's not!"

"Don't tell me what the fuck to do in my house! The house I pay the bills in. I pay the cost to be the muthafuckin' boss and, if you don't like what I say, then get the fuck out!

By now, both women were furious. Without saying a word, Harmony stormed back upstairs and burst into her bedroom. She began to pack her stuff because she couldn't find herself spending another night in what she called a hell hole.

Mahogany heard things being thrown, so she took off through the kitchen and ran upstairs. When she saw Harmony packing, she stopped her.

"Oh, hell no! That's my shit. I bought that and, if you think that I'ma let you leave to be with some thug ass nigga, then you got another thing coming!" Mahogany said as she started snatching the things she bought out of Harmony's hands.

"Mom, stop!"

They were now in a tug of war match and, after a few minutes, Harmony let go, causing her mother to fall back onto the floor. Anger was in Harmony's eyes, so she swiped everything that was on her dresser on the floor. She threw things against the wall as she huffed in puffed. Mahogany was taken aback by her outburst. She had never witnessed her daughter in such a way and she didn't want any parts of it.

"You know what; if you want that thug so bad, then get the hell out! Get the shit he bought you and get out of my damn house!" Mahogany was now getting up from the floor.

"You ain't gotta tell me twice," Harmony shot back.

She grabbed a few more of her belongings and pushed past her mother, heading down the stairs. Mahogany chased after her, just so she could continue to spew venom from her mouth.

"You got so much going for yourself and you rather be with a no-good thug. You better not bear a child by him because I tell you now. I'm not claiming those bastards..."

Mahogany got off the couch and ran into the bathroom. She looked into the mirror with disgust in her eyes and began to pull her hair.

"What the hell is wrong with you!" she cursed herself.

It had been six long years since she'd spoken to her daughter, and to know that Harmony was hurting, hurt her. She was so busy being jealous and trying to keep Harmony away from a man that completely changed since the last time she saw him. Chaos was a changed man, and Mahogany couldn't deny that. She lost so much time with her daughter and it was all her fault. There was no way she could get that time back, but the first thing she wanted to do was apologize. Harmony was her first and only child, and she disowned her as if she didn't matter.

Mahogany cleaned herself up and left out of the bathroom. She went into the kitchen and grabbed her cellphone off the countertop and went to the dial pad. She had deleted Harmony's number long ago, but she didn't forget it. After pressing in the seven-digit number, Mahogany put the phone to her ear and waited for what seemed like an eternity for Harmony to answer the phone.

Chapter Twenty-Three

Chaos Miller & Brittany:

After Chaos left Mahogany's house, he made his way to Brittany's place. He declined her offer to come to his mother's funeral because his mother wasn't feeling Brittany when she was alive, and he didn't want to disrespect her while she was gone. Chaos pulled into Burlington Manner apartment complex and parked. He couldn't believe, after all these years, Brittany was still stayed in the same place. The only difference was she upgraded her car, and that was it. Chaos didn't get out; he pulled his cellphone out and called her.

"Yo, I'm outside," he said when she answered.

"Really! I'm coming out!" she said excitedly.

Moments later, Chaos saw Brittany running towards his car. She had on a pair of all-white leggings with a pink tank top and pink sandals. The leggings hugged every curve of Brittany's so perfect body, and Chaos' dick got hard when he saw her.

"What are you doing here?" she asked when she got in the car.

"I just decided to come by and see you. I didn't want you to feel too bad that you weren't allowed at the funeral," he said.

"Ooh, well, thank you, and I'm really sorry. Even though we had our differences, Mrs. Casey was like a mother to me as well and she meant a lot to me," Brittany gave her condolences.

"Yea, I appreciate it. It's gon' take me some time to heal, but I know my mother is resting in peace right now," Chaos stated.

"You're right. Are you up to grab a bite to eat?" she asked.

"Where is your son? I never see him wit' you?" Chaos wanted to know.

"He's with my mother, big head." She gave him a playful jab. "He lives with her until I get custody back."

Chaos looked at Brittany with disappointment. He had no clue that she didn't have custody of the son she claimed was his, and she had the nerve to want to be in a relationship. It was just like Brittany to have her priorities all fucked up, which was another reason Chaos couldn't see himself being with her.

"Don't look at me like that. I had a lot of shit going on at the time. I'm getting my shit together tho," she told him.

"I would hope so. Because your son needs you," Chaos said to her.

"I know and I'ma do what I gotta do to get him back, but can we please go and get something to eat? It's going on 4 p.m. and I didn't eat anything yet," she said.

"Yea, we can go grab a bite to eat before I head back to the crib. You wanna go lock up?" he asked.

"I already did, just in case you agreed to take me to get something to eat," Brittany said as she put on her seat belt.

Chaos didn't say a word. He started up his car, put it in reverse, and backed up; he then put the car in drive and pulled out of the apartment complex. They drove silently the whole way to Golden Pigeon, which was still located in Bridgeton. Chaos had a taste for a burger and fries, so he felt like that was the perfect place to go. He pulled into the parking lot and found a close parking spot. It was always packed there, so he was surprised that he found a good spot.

Chaos shut the car off and got out. Brittany got out and hurried in front of Chaos. She switched hard and her ass jiggled as she walked. Chaos couldn't stop himself from getting aroused again. Brittany had a nice body and a nice plump ass. Her pussy wasn't better than Harmony's, but it damn sure did the job, and all he could do was picture himself giving her a nice hard pounding.

"Girl, you a trip," Chaos said and opened the door.

"A trip for you." She winked at him and walked in.

The hostess met them as they walked in and greeted them with a smile.

"Hello, table for two?" she asked.

"Yes," Brittany answered.

"Follow me," the hostess told them.

Brittany and Chaos followed the woman to their table. She sat down their menus, napkins, forks, and knives.

"Can I start you two off with anything to drink?" she asked.

"Iced tea for me and a water for him," Brittany said with a smile.

"Great, are you two ready to order?"

"I am, and I don't want a water. I want a Sprite, and I would like a cheeseburger, well done with mayonnaise, lettuce, tomato, and fried onions. Make sure my shit not burnt and make sure my fries are fresh," Chaos ordered.

Brittany was getting on his nerves, so he was becoming agitated.

"Uh, no problem sir, and for you ma'am?" She turned her attention to Brittany.

"I'll have the same thing, thank you," she said with a smile.

"Alrighty, your orders will be out soon," the woman said before taking the menus and walking away.

"What's wrong?" Brittany asked.

"You. Stop actin' like you ma girl. You about to ruin ma appetite wit' that extra shit," he told her.

Brittany rolled her eyes. "Chaos, stop tripping. I'm so tired of you dogging me like you don't want me."

Chaos ignored her. He wasn't about to argue with her in a public place or at all, for that matter. He was still grieving over his mother, and Brittany's attitude just about cut their little dinner date short.

"I'm really not even in the mood to eat anymore," Chaos said with his face tore up.

"So, what do you want to do?" Brittany asked.

"Just get ma shit to go. I'll be in the car. Hurry up so I can drop you off home." Chaos pulled out a fifty-dollar bill and left it on the table before walking out.

Brittany snatched up the money and rolled her eyes behind Chaos' back. She didn't care how much she annoyed him; she wasn't going to stop until Chaos came to his senses.

Chapter Twenty-Four

Brittany & Chaos Miller:

Brittany had invited Chaos over for a night cap. They had been spending time together for the last month or so, and she wanted that night to be the night they reconnected sexual after so many years.

"Brittany, I'm not even about to do this with you," Chaos told her.

"Boy, hush. I just wanted some company while I ate, since you cut the damn date short."

"Because you trippin'."

"Whatever Chaos. Is you gon' come in or not?" she asked.

Chaos smacked his lips before shutting off the car. He grabbed the bag of food and waited for Brittany to get out before following her to her apartment. She unlocked the door and went in; Chaos was right behind her.

"Just leave my food in the bag. I gotta run to the bathroom," she told him

"A'ight," Chaos replied.

Brittany rushed upstairs to her bedroom and took off all her clothes. While she was in the room getting dolled up for the special occasion, Chaos was downstairs sitting in her living room watching tv and eating his food. He had a found a couple of wine cooler drinks in her fridge and cracked on open.

Fifteen minutes later, Brittany came down in nothing but a red thong. Her perky titties sat up nicely and, when Chaos saw her, his dick got hard once again.

At that present time, Chaos was definitely feeling himself and he was ready to bust one, since it had been a while for him. He tried so hard to fight the temptation, but Brittany was looking too good.

"Come here," Chaos said.

Brittany didn't waste any time. She walked over to Chaos and straddled him. They began tongue kissing, as he cupped her ass and gave it a hard smack. Brittany giggled and then palmed Chaos' face with both hands.

"I missed this," she said to him.

"Yea, well, show me how much you missed this. Let me see if that mouth can still do those tricks," he said.

Brittany purred as she climbed off him and got on her knees. She unzipped his slack pants and pulled out his monster dick that she had been waiting to get a hold of since they started back talking. Brittany teased the head of Chaos' dick and then twirled her tongue around it. She made overexaggerated smacking noises before swallowing half of his dick and the spitting him back out.

"Ssss," Chaos moaned.

"You like that baby?" she asked.

"Stop all that talkin', suck this dick," he told her.

Brittany took both hands and jerked him off in a circular motion as she suck on the head. She did it at a fast pace, slowed down, then repeated it again and again. Chaos had his hand gripped on the back of her head, as he watched her and she watched him. Brittany looked Chaos deeply in his eyes before deep throating every last inch of his dick, as she cupped his balls and massaged them.

"Fuck girl!" Chaos moaned.

He couldn't take it anymore. He needed to feel Brittany's pussy walls gripping his dick. Chaos lifted her head up and then stood up. He grabbed Brittany and pushed her back on the couch and lifted her legs up. Pre-cum was oozing from the head of his penis, and Brittany's pussy was soak and wet.

"Give me that dick baby. Give me all of it," Britany moaned.

Her pussy was on fire and she wanted to feel all of Chaos at that very moment. As she pulled him close and grabbed his shaft to slide his dick in her, he pulled back.

"What the hell?" She looked at him, confused.

"I can't do this ma," Chaos said and got up.

"What the fuck you mean you can't do this?" Brittany asked.

"You know what I mean Brittany. I can't go there wit' you. We ended for a reason, and us fuckin' will only give you the assumption that I want you back and I don't," he told her.

Chaos' words hit Brittany like a ton of bricks. She fought long and hard, just to get denied by Chaos once again. Chaos could see the frustration and hurt in her face, but he didn't care. He pulled his boxer briefs back up and then his pants. He never cheated on Harmony before and he couldn't see himself starting now, especially with someone like Brittany, who didn't know how to let go. He grabbed his keys and walked to the door.

"So, that's it? You just gonna walk out on me, Chaos?" Brittany called out to him.

"Focus on gettin' ya son back Brittany. Nothin' else should matter but him," Chaos said and then walked out of her apartment, closing the door behind him.

Brittany broke down in tears when Chaos left. She thought that, after everything, Chaos would choose her, but he didn't. Her plan was to woo him in, fuck him, and get pregnant, so she could actually say he was the father of her child but, just like before, her plans backfired.

Chapter Twenty-Five

Harmony Winfield-Miller:

Harmony woke up earlier than she normally did on work days. She had a crazy dream the other night and, the moment she got to her boutique, she was going to write it down or, better yet, tell Chaos about it. The way she took it was that both her and Chaos needed to sit down and have a talk about the possibilities of what was to come, and she wanted them to be prepared for any and everything.

She sat up in the bed, stretched, and yawned while she was doing it. When she looked over at the time, it was 9:07 a.m. It wasn't like Harmony to wake up early, whether it was work days or off days. If she had to be to work at twelve o'clock on the dot, she would wake up at 11:30 a.m. and run around like a plucked chicken, trying to get herself together.

That Thursday was different from the rest because the dream cut her sleep, and the only time that ever happened was back in the day when Chaos was in the streets heavy and she worried about him like crazy. Harmony would have dreams of Chaos being shot and, sometimes, being murdered. She could remember countless times where she lost sleep because of a bad dream she had. In fact, this dream was bad, but not as bad as the ones she had in the past so that was one thing she was thankful for.

Harmony looked over at Chaos' empty spot, and she knew that he had made it to the club. It was Thursday and the club was going to be packed, but she didn't sweat it because she already knew that she would hear from her husband soon.

She crawled out of bed and headed straight for the bathroom. She peed, got up, flushed the toilet, and then turned the shower on before stripping out of her night gown she wore the night before. Harmony stepped into the shower and let the hot water run all over her chocolate skin. Just as she grabbed her washcloth, body wash, and began to wash up, she felt that she needed to use the bathroom. Trying not to lose her balance when she hopped out of the shower, Harmony plopped down on the toilet, almost sliding off from her wet bottom, and she let go.

Pwwaarrrrpppppp!

Plop!

Splash!

"Every time I wanna take a damn shower, my stomach acts up," she said out loud.

Harmony finished shitting and then grabbed one of the baby wipes out of the pack that she kept on the back of the toilet. She wiped and then flushed the toilet, before getting back in the shower. She picked up her wash rag and body wash and poured a generous amount on her rag, before putting the bottle down and washing her body good.

After the shit she took, Harmony washed up three times, just to make sure she didn't miss or leave any unwanted dirt behind. Once she was completely satisfied with her hygiene, she turned the shower off and got out. Instead of wrapping her robe around her this time, she grabbed her towel and walked out of the bathroom while she wrapped it around her wet body.

Harmony went straight to her closet and fished through tons of clothes that was hanging up, until she finally came across her outfit choice for the day. She settled for her black Burberry v-neck dress and black Christian Louboutin pumps. Once she was finished getting her outfit out, Harmony went to her dresser and grabbed some of her Shea Butter lotion and rubbed it all over her body. Once she was finished, she put on a pair of black panties and then sprayed on some perfume, along with putting on some deodorant.

After she was done making sure she smelled good and her hygiene was on point, she went ahead and got dressed. When she was finished, she looked in the mirror and unpinned her hair and let her loose curls fall past her shoulders. She freshened up her edges and applied a little lip gloss, eye liner, and eye shadow, and she was good to go. Harmony put on her pumps, grabbed her cell and bag, and she was out the door.

Beep. Beep.

Once she made sure she locked the door, she hit the unlock button on her keypad to unlock the locks on her 2014 white Chevy Impala. Harmony got in and placed her bag in the passenger seat. She connected her iPhone 6 to the aux cord and scrolled through her Apple iTunes playlist. She came across Kendrick Lamar's new song called *Humble* and turned the volume up loud. Harmony put her car in reverse and whipped out of the driveway in style. She then put the car in drive and sped down the street. She allowed her hair to blow in the wind as she made her way to her place of business.

Chapter Twenty-Six

Harmony Winfield-Miller:

Harmony Chardonnay Winfield-Miller was a beautiful sistah. Her beauty was mesmerizing. Five foot six and a petite little thing, but she held the right amount of weight in the right places. Beautiful eyes, full lips, and her silky, smooth, chocolate coco skin was radiant. Harmony was a breath of fresh air and she could have any man she wanted. She was a hard-working woman, but she couldn't front and act like she didn't use what she had to get what she wanted.

She pulled up to her business building in her all-white 2014 Chevy Impala. Harmony was twenty-seven years old and she owned her own business, which was *Love and Harmony Boutique*. She thought the name would be a perfect fit to express her love for fashion and nice things. When Harmony got out of her car, she could see through the glass windows that business was running smooth today. It was a Thursday afternoon, just days after her grand opening, and customers were already pouring in and out. She loved to see the ladies wear her latest styles in fashion. Everything was well thought out from the minds of her and approved by her love, the one and only Chaos.

"Good afternoon Mrs. Winfield," one of her workers named Crystal greeted her.

"Good afternoon honey. It looks like today is going well so far."

Crystal gave her a warm smile in response to what she said. Harmony greeted a few of her customers before heading to the back to her office. She placed her purple Tory Burch bag on her love seat before sitting down at her desk. She immediately checked her messages and missed calls. After responding back to the ones that were important, Harmony fished through the paperwork that was stacked on her desk. She had a few meetings with some important designers that she was indecisive on doing. She enjoyed doing her own thing and having her own brand, and she didn't want to gain clout off anyone else.

Ring. Ring.

Ring.

Harmony heard the ringing of her phone and slid her swivel chair back. She got up and went to her bag and pulled out her cellphone. Her heart melted when she saw Chaos' picture flash across the screen, along with his name.

"Hello handsome," she purred.

"What it do beautiful?" His deep voice made her heart do a special melody for him.

Harmony sat back down at her desk. "Nothing much. I'm just sitting here going through some paperwork. I have to order a few more things for the store, clothing included."

"Well, I'll be over there shortly, so we can discuss all that needs to be ordered, ight?"

Harmony blushed. She loved how Chaos was always ready to cater to her every need. It was just like him to be at his place of business, but drop everything when it came to her.

"Okay handsome. I'll see you soon," she purred.

"Ight bae."

Click.

Chaos ended the call and got up from his swivel chair. He closed his laptop and made sure his office was straight and the cameras were catching everything before he shut off the light and walked out. He walked into the club area and waved towards his right-hand, Brave, to grab his attention.

Brave ended his conversation when one of the bouncers followed Chaos outside. It was the afternoon, but the club was packed.

"Wassup, bruh?" Brave asked.

"I'm about to run to Harmony's boutique and help her out there for a few. I need you to hold things down, ya feel me?"

Brave leaned his head back. "Nigga, now you know I'm always on my P's and Q's when it come to our business. You know damn well I got shit down pack when you here or if you not. Me nor Coroner gon' allow anything to go unnoticed or pop off. Go handle ya business, and tell sis I said what's up," he assured.

Chaos laughed. "I know, I know, but I still like to make sure ya hot headed ass gon' be good before I dip off."

"Nah, everything gon' be good. These niggas just better know that I don't mind puttin' a muthafuckin' bullet in a nigga if need be," Brave stated seriously.

Chaos nodded in agreement. "I feel you but, ight, let me go head and get goin'. I'm check you in a few. Hit me if anything, ya heard?" Chaos gave Brave dap before jogging to his car.

Brave made sure Chaos was in his car safe before heading back into the club.

***

Chaos Miller:

Chaos made it to Harmony's boutique in no time. He pulled right in back of her car and parked. He got out and people noticed him immediately.

"Hey Chaos."

"How you doing handsome? Ya club be poppin'. You'll definitely see me soon as my check come."

"Chaos, when you gon' stop playing!"

Different females were trying to have a conversation with him all at once, but he kept walking, ignoring them like he normally did. When he walked into the store, he was greeted by Crystal, who always worked the front register.

"Hey, Mr. Miller. How are you today?" she asked.

"I'm good, how you?" he asked, giving her the same respect she had just given him.

"I'm just fine. Your wife is in the back," she said.

"I know, but thanks for the confirmation. Wassup Jasmin." He turned his attention to another worker at the store.

"Hello, how are you?" she asked with a warm smile.

"Ain't no thang, everything is all good. Had to come by and help the wife with a few things. You good?" he asked.

"Yes, I'm blessed, you know that." She smiled.

Chaos nodded and shook his head at Renee, who was popping gum loud.

"Girl, you forever extra," he laughed.

"Shut up, ya boy love it!" she laughed back.

"Yea, he the only one that can tolerate ya crazy ways. How you doin' tho?" he asked.

"I'm good. Just trying to make sure everything runs smoothly today. Business has been booming and the grand opening was just a few days ago. I'm proud of her," she said.

"Me too. She deserves everything God is blessing her with," Chaos responded.

"She sure does; now, you better get back there in that office before she bites all of our heads off," Renee stated.

Chaos put his hands up in defense as he laughed. He turned around and walked to the office. He walked straight in and found Harmony typing on her computer.

"Wassup beautiful," he greeted as he walked around the desk to kiss her.

"Hey handsome. Thank you for coming," she said.

Chaos waved her off. "What you sayin' thank you for, when I'm doing something I'm supposed to do."

Harmony blushed. "You are too much. My mind has been roaming since the grand opening and, once I got here, I just sat down and started randomly writing."

Chaos sat down on one of her plush love seats and kicked off his sneakers. "Writing what?" he asked in curiosity.

"You sure you want to know?"

"Of course, you know we don't keep secrets from one another."

Harmony smirked before she spoke again and, the more she talked, the more Chaos was in awe with how vivid her mind was.

***

Chaos Miller & Harmony Winfield-Miller:

An hour or so later, Chaos sat in awe as Harmony laughed at his facial expression. He couldn't believe that she had told him such a story and damn near tried to predict their future. He was impressed and uneasy all in one.

"So, what do you think?" Harmony asked.

Chaos shook his head. "Now, why the fuck would you tell me a story like that?" he asked in confusion.

"Bae, because anything could happen. Like, do you really think we are prepared for what's to come?" she asked.

Chaos wiped his hands down his face.

"You know how much shit we've been through? Of course, we're ready. This is what we were put here to do. God knew that we were going to be CEO's of our own businesses one day, and here it is. But, although we were blessed don't mean I won't knock ya fuckin' head loose if you ever think about pulling some shit like the bullshit you just spoke of."

Chaos was as serious as a heart attack. He understood what she was trying to say, but the way she delivered it was mind boggling as hell to him.

"Baby, I would never cheat on you. I was just saying like what if the club took you away from me? What if the life you lived in the past came back to haunt you? What if, just what if?" she said.

Chaos sighed.

"First and foremost, stop with the what if's because that's how shit goes left. Secondly, ain't no bitch or nigga stupid enough to go to war with me. Thirdly, no matter how mad you get with me, the word bitch ain't comin' outta my mouth when it comes to you. The shit about ya mother was true, and we need to really fix it ASAP. Yawl haven't talked in years and life is really too short. And Lord knows I pray to God my mother ain't holding no secrets like that either. The only sibling I know is Boots and, the way you flipped, that shit got my mind runnin' wild, but moving on. Brittany never was and never will be an issue. She was just a fuck back then, and she ain't never gettin' none of this big black dick again, and we all know that the baby she had wasn't mines. I'm bussin' ya guts down and only ya guts, so don't ever think that another bitch would get this big muthafucka, but what I do like is how you predicted the way Brave and Renee could've met. That shit was tight," he chuckled.

"Yea, it's crazy how I came up with that, but the good part about it is that they're together, and he completely changed her life. Who would've thought that they would have connected the way that they did just days after your grand opening. It's been what, for them? Eight months, and they're still going steady. I'm proud of them but, most of all, I'm proud of you. Not only has your club been open for a total of seven months, but you did it on your own with the help of Brave and Coroner, of course, but that's not the point, you know what I mean," she explained.

Chaos peeped how she didn't continue to touch basis on her mother. He respected it for now, but he made a mental note to come at her later concerning it.

"I feel you and everything you sayin', but I doubt if any of that or anything like that happens. We been through hell and back and I did my dirt in the past, just as well as you did yours. I'm thankful that you never went as far as me, but you get where I'm going with this. I understand we gonna have trials and tribulations, but it ain't nothin' we can't handle. I'm made of steel baby; I'm a lion, and you my lioness."

Harmony rolled her eyes but couldn't hide the fact that she was blushing. It was just like Chaos to always turn her partially negative thoughts into positive ones. She loved that man with everything inside of her, and cheating on him wasn't even an option. He was a workaholic but, when it came to her, he would drop everything without hesitation. She couldn't have asked for a better husband. By no means was Chaos perfect, but he was her husband and she loved him flaws and all. He changed tremendously from his younger days and until now, and she knew that he changed for her, as well as wanting to change for the better.

Harmony took the dream she had as an eye opener for both of them. She looked at it as, no matter how hard things got for them, neither one of them should turn their backs on one another or feel so alone to where they seek love elsewhere. They were both bosses now, and she was well aware that shit could get hectic, but she had to be prepared for anything.

"What are you over there thinking about?" she asked, snapping Chaos out of his train of thought.

"Just wondering how much of a story that Brave and Renee had to tell." He shrugged his shoulders.

Harmony placed her elbow on her desk and her hand under her chin, as she thought for second. Brave and Renee had a crazy relationship. They were both hood as hell and came from nothing fighting for something. Two bull-headed people in a relationship was bound to be one bumpy ass rollercoaster.

"Damn, that would be one hell of a story."

THE END

Questions For Readers & Book Club

1. What did you think of the outcome of the story?

2. Did you expect the twist and turns?

3. Do you understand where Harmony was coming from?

4. Do you feel like any of what happened will become reality for the married couple?

5. How did you feel when you found out Kaotic was just a dream?

6. Do you think Harmony and her mother Mahogany will finally make amends?

7. Did you really think Chaos and Brittany had a baby?

8. Do you think the advice Casey gave Chaos was good motherly advice?

9. What do you think Brave and Renee have in store for you all?

Get the entire
HARMONY & CHAOS COLLECTION
Today!

Available Now!
www.iamredsjohnson.com

Reds Johnson also known as Anne Marie, is a twenty-three-year-old independent author born and raised in New Jersey. She started writing at the age of nine years old, and ever since then, writing has been her passion. Her inspirations were Danielle Santiago, and Wahida Clark. Once she came across their books; Reds pushed to get discovered around the age of thirteen going on fourteen.

To be such a young woman, the stories she wrote hit so close to home for many. She writes urban, romance, erotica, bbw, and teen stories and each book she penned is based on true events; whether she's been through it or witnessed it. After being homeless and watching her mother struggle for many years, Reds knew that it was time to strive harder. Her passion seeped through her pores so she knew that it was only a matter of time before someone gave her a chance.

Leaping head first into the industry and making more than a few mistakes; Reds now has the ability to take control of her writing career. She is on a new path to success and is aiming for bigger and better opportunities.

Visit my website www.iamredsjohnson.com

MORE TITLES BY REDS JOHNSON

SILVER PLATTER HOE 6 BOOK SERIES

HARMONY & CHAOS 6 BOOK SERIES

MORE TITLES BY REDS JOHNSON

NEVER TRUST A RATCHET BITCH 3 BOOK SERIES

TEEN BOOKS

A PROSTITUTE'S CONFESSIONS SERIES

CLOSED LEGS DON'T GET FED SERIES

MORE TITLES BY REDS JOHNSON

OTHER TITLES BY REDS JOHNSON